9/13

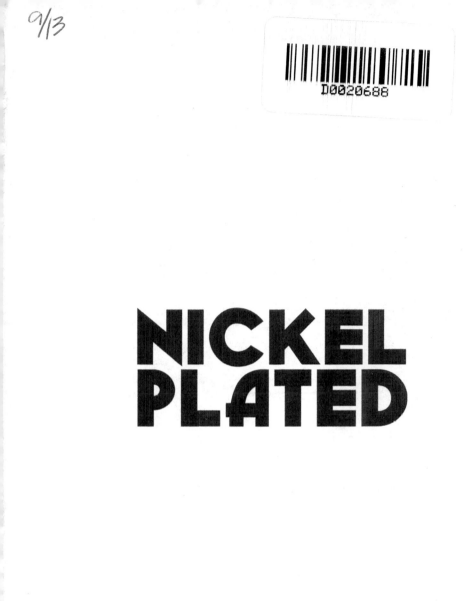

NICKEL PLATED

NICKEL PLATED

ARIC DAVIS

PUBLISHED BY

amazon encore

The characters and events portrayed in this book are fictitious. Any similarity to real persons, living or dead, is coincidental and not intended by the author.

Published by AmazonEncore
P.O. Box 400818
Las Vegas, NV 89140

ISBN-13: 978-1-935597-32-2
ISBN-10: 1-935597-32-9

Dedicated to Sara Dobbrastine, Julie Hatch, and Jonel Hoogterp—strong women taken before their time.

Chapter 1

She said that she needed help. I told her that Facebook chat was not the way to contact someone like me. (It was a dummy account, but still.) I gave her my pager number. When it buzzed a few seconds later, I grabbed my phone and plugged in cord number six, the Trans' line. They don't mind me using their landline because they don't know. I dialed as quickly as the rotary dial would allow, and she answered on the first ring.

"Hello?"

"What do you want?"

"Is this..."

"Yes. No names on the phone. You know where Riverside Park is?"

"Yes, but..."

"Meet me there, one hour. There's a playground by a bridge, and you'll know you're in the right spot because there will be a man on a different bench with gray hair and an eyepatch. I'm not him, and he will not talk to you. I'll be on a green bench across from him, by the swings. Come alone and wear a red top."

I put the phone back on the receiver and headed to my bedroom for a costume change. The house is a pit. Someday when I have time, I'll get around to cleaning it. I don't anticipate that day

1

coming anytime soon. The place is perfect for me, a two-bedroom with an attached garage and a finished basement. I have an office in the larger of the two bedrooms, and the other one is where I sleep. To say I could use some furniture would be an understatement.

To live like I do for very long you have to look the part out in the world, and today I needed to blend as smooth as a KitchenAid. It was weird to just get a contact out of nowhere; I usually get some kind of a heads-up about what to expect and who made the referral. She was a kid, though, I could tell that from just the few minutes on the phone, and kids have a funny way of finding me. I'm pretty sure it's just the world's way of reminding me that I owe a debt for Dad. Whoever the girl was, she either needed help or was setting me up. I don't know that anyone is after me, but I've run enough angles that I'm sure there are a few people who'd love to get a face-to-face. I'll die before I go back to any kind of foster care, and I'm not ready to start dying just yet.

Like I said, job one in avoiding that is to fit in. That day that meant Levi's and a shirt from Aéropostale. Kids today have no fashion sense, and believe me, if the costume weren't necessary, it's about the last thing I'd be caught wearing. Orphaned, short for my age, and red-headed, life has been cruel enough already.

In another minute I was on the street, just another twelve-year-old on a mountain bike. It looked ratty, but it was a five-thousand-dollar machine that had been fine-tuned to look like the crap you might buy at Wal-Mart and leave in the yard a few times a week. The park wasn't far, but I wanted to be early.

Riverside Park is two entirely different places. At night it's a circle of hell close to the inferno. A couple of years ago, there were dead prostitutes turning up like old relatives at Christmas dinner, and you wouldn't see anybody in there after dusk. Daytime though, whole other story. Moms and babies and unsupervised kids running around in a manner that made me wish for stricter leash laws. When they finally busted the guy doing in the hookers, it was during the day. Nobody even batted an eye.

I parked my bike and wrapped a chain around the frame to make it look like it was locked up. If I needed to go, I didn't want to mess with undoing a lock; if it got stolen, I'd buy another one. Business expense. The bench I sat at was different than the one I told the girl about. It was a little bit away from the playground, but I could see over there just fine. I could see Eyepatch and the swings and everything else. Today I saw a teenage girl wearing a red sweater and a pair of jeans. I walked over to her and said, "Hey."

"Go away."

"This is a public park."

She was prettier than she'd sounded on the phone. Strawberry blonde with violent red highlights, pretty nice set of cans from what I could tell through the sweater. Hey, I'm twelve, not blind. I smiled and she scowled back.

"I don't care what it is; leave me alone."

"I thought you needed help."

Her mouth formed an O. I really couldn't blame her for being surprised.

"You're Nickel?"

"Yep. And you're about a dime."

She blushed. Girls are all the same. "You're just a kid."

"So are you. You're what, fourteen?"

She eyed me and then walked past me and sat down hard on one of the swings. I sat on the one next to her, letting my Converses drag in the wood chips. (Shirt and pants are one thing—I pick the kicks I want to wear.)

"You're just a kid. I heard you could help. When I asked around, like really asked, they said to ask for Nickel. Are you like his younger brother or something?"

"Babe, I've got a lot of stuff I could be doing right now, and that's not your fault, but if you don't tell me what you want, I'm going to get working on some of it."

She looked sad, and I tried to look like I cared.

"It's my sister."

"What about her?"

They always think I'm a mind reader. I'm not, but I'll admit I'd do a good impression if somebody asked.

"She's missing."

"Runaway?"

"I don't think so, but that's what my mom and dad think."

"How long has she been gone?"

"Three days."

"They file her as a missing person?"

"I think so."

"Tell me about her."

"Her name is Shelby. She's eleven, and the last time anybody saw her she was riding her bike to the library. She has green eyes, hair the same color as mine, without the red, and she's about five feet tall."

"She have any issues with anybody?"

"No. Who would have any real issues with an eleven-year-old?"

I grimaced. This was a conversation this chick would not want to have with me. There were a pile of kids that age and younger that I knew of who'd died because somebody had issues with them—usually an adult, sometimes a kid their age, sometimes a kid younger.

"Any pervs in your neighborhood?"

"No. We live in Four Oaks."

"So they'd be rich pervs. You do a search for any?"

"What do you mean?"

Kids today.

"Go to Google and type in 'search for Michigan sex offenders.' There's a whole database for the ones who have gotten caught, and believe me, these sickos are too stuck thinking about what's in their pants to worry about how risky getting what they think they need can be. I'll look for you; give me your address."

"1138 Oakway." She looked at me expectantly and then said, "Aren't you going to write it down?"

"If I needed to, I would." So maybe I showed off a little—sue me.

"Do you have a phone number I can call you at?"

"Nope, the pager works just fine. You won't need to anyways—I'll find you."

I walked two steps from her and then turned back. "I never caught your name."

"Arrow. Like bow and arrow."

"All right, Arrow, nice to meet you. Like I said, I'll be in touch."

I walked away from her, and away from my bike. I gave Eyepatch a wave, but he didn't wave back. He never does. That's okay—he's here to relax just like everybody else. Doesn't mean I can't extend the courtesy. I heard a rumor once that Eyepatch used to be a lawyer, a prosecutor who got sick of all the crap that comes along with that line of work, and now he spends time here, feeding the birds. Fair enough. He gives off absolutely no perv vibes, and that's all I care about, especially for a guy spending his days gazing out across a playground. Whatever wheels are turning in there, they don't look like crazy ones to me, so he gets a wave.

I looped around the outside of the park and didn't catch any scent of being followed. Saw one weirdo sitting on a bench enjoying a hearty game of pocket pool. At least he was by the jogger's track and not the playground. In fifteen minutes I was on my bike and ghosted.

Chapter 2

When I first ran away from foster care, I was eight. I had no idea what I was doing or where I would go. When I was ten, after being passed around like a thick joint in a frat house, I ended up with the Richardsons. Sam and Kathy. Sweet deal at first—they were just as nice as could be. The other two kids, Eleanor and Nicholas, were quiet, reserved all the time. At first I thought they just didn't like me, so I kept away and stuck to myself. Like I said, it was a good gig. Hot, home-cooked meals, the house wasn't overcrowded, and I had my own room! Believe me, I'd put up with worse than two kids who think they're better than me just because they've been somewhere longer. Sometimes a lot worse.

After being there a few months, I was as high on the hog as I can remember being since Dad died. I should have been seeing warning signs going off all around me, but I was just too comfortable to care. Dad had taught me better than that, and I owed him sharper eyes and ears than I showed during that time. When it all fell apart, it fell apart fast.

Nicky cornered me one afternoon and told me that I was getting a girlfriend. I laughed, probably told him that he was stupid or gay or something. He just looked at me with these cold eyes, and I thought about how I'd never seen his or Eleanor's rooms before, and about how when I was busy with my stuff, there was never anyone else around.

When I woke up the next morning, I learned a lot.

I was watching TV with Nick and Eleanor; I'm pretty sure it was a *Simpsons* rerun. In any case, Sam came into the house with a little girl in tow. She was Guatemalan, he said, and she was named Annette. Kathy was right behind them, smiling. She said it was time for the six of us to go to the basement.

I'd been told since day one that I was not to go in the basement. I'd never even wondered about it, or about how we were homeschooled and how I hadn't left the house since I'd walked into it in the first place. All these questions popped into my head at once as Sam made me hold hands with Annette and follow him down the stairs. I could hear the rest of them stomping behind me as we went to the basement.

The basement was like no room I'd ever seen. Every corner seemed to hold something different. All I could think of was that it was like how I'd always imagined a movie set would be. There were bits and pieces of little worlds hung on hooks and on shelves all over the basement. I could see parts of an Arabian-looking desert area with a painted background, a living room that was a miniature of the one upstairs, complete with matching, albeit smaller, furniture. Parts from an auto mechanic's shop, the chalkboard from a schoolroom, a mattress and box spring that matched the one in my bedroom, and a few more I can't remember. At the center of it all, there was a video camera on a tripod. I do remember Kathy leaning down and asking me in a voice I'd never heard before where I wanted Annette's and my date to be. I didn't say anything. Sam pulled Annette away from me and started stripping off her clothing. Kathy was walking around the basement lighting candles, and Eleanor and Nick just stood there looking miserable. I could see from looking at them that they knew all too well what was going on. I could see that they'd been on a few dates too.

What happened next was a mess, but it left me alive and on the run. I try and think of Nick and Eleanor every day. NickEl. I wish Annette had lived long enough to help us escape.

Chapter 3

When I got home, I parked the bike in the garage and went out back to water the garden. It truly is amazing how well marijuana is disguised by corn. I've never smoked the stuff, my crop or anybody else's, but from what I hear I do a pretty good job at growing it. I turned the faucet on and let the little sprinklers I'd staked out take care of the rest. I waited for five minutes and thought about what Arrow had said. Nothing was even close to coming up, so I shut off the water and went inside. I plugged my pager into its charger and took the steps downstairs.

My basement is unfinished, and I plan to keep it that way. It's where I dry all the dope, and believe me, the stink from that needs to be contained. When I first started, you could smell the skunky reek a few doors down. I reevaluated and sold the lot of it for cheap, did some work with dryer exhaust systems, and planted a ton of Thai basil around them in the yard. No problem with odor ever since. I had about nine pounds drying; it was a slow summer, and I had a little bit of a bug issue. I moved some of it around so that the fans would get all the sides and went back up after I shut off the lights.

I was hungry, so I made a couple of peanut butter and jellies, finished them quickly, put my pager in my pocket, and went back to the garage to get my bike. It was already getting cold. I looked at my watch—almost five. I shut the garage door behind me with the clicker and left.

The post office is only about five minutes away, and I like to try and go every day. Someday I'll get a car and everything will be that convenient, but I have four years to wait on that, and the last thing I need before that happens is to get pulled over for something dumb. I'll set up the legit fake when I'm sixteen, through the mail and with a different name. I parked my bike, stuck it in the rack, and did my thing with the chain. I left the bike and walked inside, the doors opening for me like I was royalty. I wasn't, just some dumb kid who needed a shower, and maybe a hug. I knew I'd be getting one of them soon enough and that the other one was a fair shot away.

There was a line stretching right to the door of civilians holding packages and looking bored. I watched in a way that would make it hard to tell that I was watching, and when I didn't see anybody interested in some random kid, I went to the side lobby where the PO boxes are. I checked the area and then moved to my box as fast as I could without running. I took another good look around before I stuck my key in, emptied the box, and blew out of there. Three envelopes, no return addresses. Looked like payday came early. I took the chain off my bike, stuck the envelopes in my pocket with my pager, and rode around aimlessly for a while—stupid kid stuff. Sometimes that's the easiest thing to forget, how to be what I'm supposed to be.

I walked in through the garage, but I waited until I was in the house to open the envelopes. Two cashier's checks for a grand each and one for eight hundred. Messrs. Hotforlove, Boy-Friend, and LookingtoLurn had all paid up. Not surprisingly, none had left a return address. Oh well, if I needed their names or addresses, I had them. If these guys would just think, even a little bit, life would be infinitely more affordable for them, certainly easier than getting scammed by me or tossed in the can and thrown to the wolves in general population. In any case, I put the checks in my office and stripped down to my boxers, and then I put on some pajama pants. Tried not to think about how most kids my age had a parent pick out pajama pants, maybe still called them pj's. Mine were camouflage; I bought them at the army surplus store, and I'm pretty sure they're just comfortable, and not pajamas.

I hopped on the computer, checked my Facebook and my MySpace, checked the dummy e-mail accounts that I have, and even checked the encrypted real one. Nothing, at least nothing that mattered. I hopped on the Michigan sex offender database and entered Arrow and Shelby's address. Loaded another window, started lining up "curious tween" chat rooms. Entered as shyBoy on all of them. Threw some hooks out. Went fishing. There'd be lots of bites. There always are.

I turned up three sex offenders within a ten-mile radius of Arrow and Shelby's home address, and about a hundred and fifty within a twenty-five-mile scan. I thought about doing my own address again, but it had only been a couple of days. My neighborhood sees about a ten-mile radius of nothing. You're welcome, neighbors. Arrow and Shelby's neighborhood was a lot of research all on its own, and I hadn't even talked the reality of this thing over with Arrow. The site was the first place to check, but chances were it wouldn't be a listed offender. I clicked on some sicko in the second scan. No luck, he'd only been busted for raping grown women. The next two had a kick for boys. Why is it that two-thirds of these guys have smiles on their faces in their mug shots?

Fourth one panned out. Had a jones for the minors, third-degree sexual assault with a girl under twelve. Gave the profile a look—too quick. Missed the birthdate on the first pass, but caught it on the second. Poor kid was fourteen, and the girl was a week from twelve. From the sound of things, he got caught touching what passed for her breasts; she was good with it, but her mom wasn't. I went back to work.

The next three hits were all within thirteen miles of the house. Same trailer park and same trailer. Three for the price of one? Nope. Halfway trailer I guess, home for nut jobs, and these three were in it. I e-mailed the page to myself but wrote it off inside; halfway houses never panned out. I took a break, went back to my lines. Lots of nibbles, no bites. My pager yelled in my pants. I checked it: Gary, 400. Four ounces, not a bad night. I shut the chats, threw a forty-mile search on the address, and went to the basement. I grabbed four ounces of pot and went back to the garage. Opened it and rode my bike into the blackness.

The high school was about as far away as the post office, but riding at night made it go much faster. Too many four-way stops on the route, and too many people who didn't understand how they worked. At night it was a cruise, a spy mission on my mountain bike, black mag wheels and secrets as deep as the Marianas. I rode, my backpack full of pot and my mind full of missing sisters, my heart full of nothing.

I left the pot in the electrical box that I'd put in before I'd first spoken to Gary. I'd done my homework on him, knew everything about him. All he knew about me was that I sold him pot. The electrical box was easy; I bought tin, put it together, and painted it green. Stuck it on a corner by the high school one night and planted a shrub by it. The box was bolted to some four-by-fours and opened with a button on the opposite side of the lock, but no one from the school had ever checked it as far as I knew. Either way, it was just further proof of the mindset in most civilians: why even question a thing like the electric company stealing some space in your yard?

Last year, Gary was one of the nerdiest kids in Northland High School; this year, he could pull off prom king if he wanted to. Gary had been my project a year and a half ago, and no project of mine has ever turned out better. I think I'd like Gary, and maybe someday I'll even meet him.

Gary's issue was his mom. She was destroying his life and had been on a steady path for what I assume was forever, a nice mixed diet of hardcore born-again thinking and a set of rules so strict it made Jackson Penitentiary look like summer camp. He was trying to take it in stride as a good boy should, but I could see something more than his yearbook photo was willing to tell me. It wasn't just the lonely-looking Facebook account covered in tired memes, but missing friends; there was something more there, something I could see that was desperate to break free. I reached out, on a burner cell phone that had limited texting. I sent him a message: "Call this number if you want to have a life." He paged me, and the rest is history. I've got my dopeboy, and he's got his source.

Gary stopped being a nerd when he drove his Mustang to prom and had two dates on his arms that he pried off of a stripper pole. He was a junior and even the teachers gave him respect. Gary owed me, but he'd never need to cover the debt—beyond selling my pot and making us both a good sum of money. My sum was better, of course. Today my take was just over three thousand dollars.

I whistled while I rode my bike home, but it wasn't to keep up appearances. It was just for me.

Chapter 4

I woke up at about seven and made some eggs on the stove. If there's one thing I hate about not being able to drive, it's buying groceries. I can't take a cab every time I go to the store, it would be too conspicuous, which means I'm really limited to what I can carry in my backpack. I used to eat out, but after noticing how people were looking at me, I stopped. A kid should be able to take himself out for a steak dinner if he wants to, regardless of his age. I ate the eggs and checked my pager; Arrow had called, and so had a number I didn't know. I rinsed the plate and threw it in the dishwasher.

I have eight different phone lines that I use, all connected to my neighbors' houses. It was actually a pretty easy hustle—not as easy as stealing Wi-Fi, but other than actually hooking up to their houses, it was a risk-free venture. I made sure to never make more than a couple of phone calls a month per line, and I always kept them as short as possible. When I first started I was using a burner all the time, and then I read about how easy it was to intercept a signal. That was enough for me. I just waited until people went on vacation, and then I put on my lifted boots and my phone company suit. There was a time when neighbors were friendly enough that they would have discussed the phone company digging in their yard while they were out of town. Fortunately for me, those days were long gone.

I called Arrow on line two. I put my feet on my computer desk and looked at the forty-mile ring on the screen. A sea of registered offenders had popped up. How many unregistered? How many that had never been caught? I shut the browser tab as the phone rang—forty miles was just too far. I was working the ten-mile when she answered.

"Hello?"

"You called."

"Is this…"

"Don't. Got school today?"

"Yeah."

"Meet me in the park, same spot, four o'clock. You remember?"

"Yes."

I hung up the phone. If Arrow thought this was going to go that fast, she was in for a rude awakening. I looked at my pager, plugged in line seven on the rotary, and dialed. A woman's voice answered.

"Hello?"

"You paged me."

"Oh."

"Downtown library. Main floor. Fiction. I'll be holding a book by Joe R. Lansdale. Wear a green dress so I know it's you. If you don't have a green dress, then wear green and get a book by Dan Simmons before you walk to Lansdale. One hour."

"What?"

"One hour."

I hung up the phone. Good thing I ate before I called. I checked my chat logs for shyBoy. Too bad I'd fallen asleep—there had been sharks out last night. There would be more tonight.

I showered, dressed in jeans and a shirt that said "Hollister" across the front, and pulled on my All-Stars. I signed the backs of the cashier's checks, hopped on my bike, and rode downtown. My bank was on the way, so I stopped there first, throwing the checks in the drop-off box with a deposit slip. I glanced at my watch and saw I had fifteen minutes. I put the pedal to the metal, baby—keeping in mind, of course, that the metal in this case tends to oscillate.

I was at the library in five minutes. If I were smarter, I'd have remembered I had stuff to return. The sad price of too much on my plate. Oh well. I parked my bike, made a big show of wrapping a chain around the frame, and climbed the stone steps to the front door. I walked in, nodded at the guy working the front desk, and strolled into fiction. I went straight to Lansdale and grabbed *Freezer Burns*; I've read it five or six times, but a couple more pages wouldn't hurt anything. She came around the corner just a few minutes after I picked up the book.

I really need to grow up, I thought.

She had on a green dress, and I was pretty happy I'd said dress and not sweatshirt. She had curves in all the right places, and even though she was old enough to be my mom, I got myself an eyeful. Some things age well, and she was one of them. The dress was perfectly contoured to her body, and her feet were impossibly balanced on stiletto heels. She had short red hair that looked natural but might have been dyed; I knew I wouldn't be finding out which one anytime soon. She looked predictably startled when she saw me. Dealing with that was the least of my issues. I pushed

Freezer Burns back onto the shelf, extended a hand, and said, "I'm Nickel."

She took my hand and shook it twice; it came back smelling like perfume, and not the kind from a drugstore.

"Nice to meet you. I'm Veronica."

"Should we tour the library grounds, Veronica?"

It was kind of a joke. The closest thing to grounds the library has is a park dedicated to veterans where bums sleep. I thought a little hike in the concrete jungle would be more appropriate. I walked past the park and the old YMCA building and led her next to an old stone church. When we were by the steps, I slowed to walk with her instead of leading her and asked her who'd told her about me.

"So you really are Nickel? No offense, but I'm not hiring some kid."

If I had a nickel.

"Look, Veronica? I don't care if you want to hire me or not; I just want to know who told you about me. If you've got work for me, great, but if not, I've got other fish to fry."

She looked at me kind of pouty. I'm the kid, and she's the one acting like one. "I heard about you from a guy I work with named Mikey. He said you did some work for him that helped with his divorce."

I had done some work with Mikey; I slashed his wife's lover's tires so that he could catch the two in the act.

"He never mentioned you were a kid."

"Then he followed the rules; good on him. You have a nice day, Veronica." I turned to walk back to the library, barely made it two feet, and she was next to me. I stopped and said, "What now?"

"Don't you want to hear what I have to say?"

"Aren't I just a kid?"

"I'm sorry about that." She started crying, and I almost felt bad. It passed. She snuffled and said, "It's my son. He's in eleventh grade, and he goes to Forest Hills High School. He's dating a girl and I just can't stand her."

"What can I do about that?"

"She's got him out with a bad group—drinking, fighting, I don't even know what. He was fine before this girl, but now it's like I don't even know my own son. I just want him back to how he was."

"What if it's not the girl?"

"How do you mean?"

"I mean, what if this was your son all along and he just found out?"

"You don't know Jeff. That's not what he's like."

"It sounds like he's doing a good impersonation."

I stuck a matchstick in my mouth and gave her my cool look, but it came off a little sour, more pickle than cucumber. She gave me the eyes right back, and I said, "I'll give him a look. Hundred bucks a day. Give me three days to figure out what his deal is." I handed her a piece of paper with a post office box number on it, a different box than the one for my perv scam. "You get me the three hundred, cashier's check made out to cash. I'll start Thursday, try and have his kick figured out by Saturday night. Once I know what the deal is, we can work on fixing the problem."

"How much will that cost?"

"No clue. When I know, you will. What's Jeff's last name?"

"Rogers."

"It was a pleasure to meet you, Veronica. I'll talk to you soon."

I shook her hand again and walked away. I could feel her eyes on me as I pounded pavement. If I were a little taller, darker, or handsomer, she'd probably be thinking about getting that hot detective into the sack with her. Instead she had me: short, ginger, and maybe not too ugly, patch of freckles where a scar ought to be and a lean body that came from getting my butt kicked at Rhino's Gym, not a high metabolism. She didn't know it, but my specs beat out tall, dark, and handsome any day. Nobody expects anything out of a kid.

I unhooked the chain and decided to bike on over to Four Oaks. It was near enough to the park, and I still had some time to kill. I hopped on the bike and got pedaling.

My city passes by me in the wind; I just hope it ignores me as well as I act like I'm ignoring it. The sun's already drooping in the west—just like the wind, it's trying to tell me the snow is on the way. I can feel eyes tugging at me, wondering why I'm not in school. As long as none of those eyes wear a badge, I'm good to go. I ride through the city and into suburbia—just as many eyes, but twice the secrets. When I get to Four Oaks, I'm sweaty but smiling. There's a cool breeze, a reward. I drop to a lower gear and start coasting.

I found 1138 Oakway without much work. Nice house, big yard, and well kept too. If it wasn't missing a child, it would have been just fine. It would have been honest to sit Arrow down and talk statistics, specifically on the chances of her sister surviving being kidnapped by a stranger. I set the thought aside. It might have been honest, but it would have been cruel. It was bad her sister was taken; it was worse to say that chances are she'd died bad and would never be found, and if she were found it would be by some very unlucky hikers. I rested atop my bike for a moment and then adjusted my trek to head to the library. Not the one I'd met Veronica at, but a small suburban branch. I got pedaling, slow like, but not too slow. I wanted to be the predator, not the prey.

I took the little notepad that I keep in my back pocket and made myself zero in, focus on little things that seemed out of place. A house with three sheds, a mansion with no landscaping, anything that seemed out of the cardboard cutout standard of the rest of the neighborhood. The little bit of adult in me was screaming that freaks hid in normalcy, but I couldn't help but look for the odd stuff first; there was too much normal to see much odd anyways. I crossed through some heavier woods, over a small bridge, and out of the suburbs. A gas station, crossing light, and a sign for the library met me. I turned around to ride back and give a look again when the bridge hit me funny. I walked the bike back, leaned it on the steel guardrail, and sat next to it. There was something just off about the spot. There was a grooved trail that I could tell had been carved by bicycles, but there was new grass in the trail, so it had been a little while since it had been used. The spot was perfect if your goal was to abduct someone; not a single car had passed since I'd stopped. I looked back at my bike, then into the woods again. There was some matted grass on the right side of the path. Someone had been there recently, and it wasn't an animal bedding down—this was too close to a road for that.

That's when I saw a flash of pink beyond that patch of flattened grass—farther down the trail, almost to the creek. Something was down there. I left my bike and jumped the guardrail.

Whatever I'd seen, it was wind that had showed it to me, so I tried to keep in line with where my bike was above me. I went slowly, let focus remain and let everything else slide out of me. I stumbled but stayed my course. The wind rewarded me because I was a good boy, and I walked to it. It was a pink hair band, big enough for a girl about Shelby's age. Next to it in the mud was an enormous boot print. It was intricate, and I made a little sketch in my notepad. There were deep grooves in the middle of it, almost as though someone had stuck a spike through the center of the shoe print. I picked up the hair band and shook mud off of it. In addition to being pink, there were some dark red spots on one side. I didn't figure it was a pattern. I felt watched as I left the creek and biked to the park.

I was early by a couple of hours, but I didn't care. I brought the hair band with me to the bench and waved at Eyepatch. He didn't wave back. I sat and dozed off. Stupid. When I woke, I was sitting on the bench with the hair band in a clenched fist on my chest. In my dream a demon with a face from the blackest pits of my memory was chasing me, but my feet were stuck in mud. I took a deep breath, cleared the thoughts, and waited for Arrow. Four o'clock on the nose, she was there. I let her come to me.

She was wearing a short blue and green plaid skirt, a white button-up blouse, a short tie to match the skirt, and a gray sweater. She sat next to me on the bench. I could smell her perfume, and it was nice. I wanted to wrap my arms around her, but we really didn't have that kind of relationship. I said, "You didn't mention the private school."

"Didn't think I needed to."

I smiled, she didn't. Arrow was probably running out of smiles. I handed her the hair band. "Recognize this?"

"Where did you find that? Shelby has one just like this!"

"You know if she was wearing it the day she disappeared?"

"No, I have no idea, but she could have been. I'll check her room. Where did you find it?"

"By the creek a couple of miles from your house. I rode down to the library and then back again. Found it on the way back."

"Was there anything else?"

I thought about the boot print and said, "No, just that."

She started crying then. I thought about reaching out to take her hand, but like she said, I was just a kid. I let her cry, and she sniffled and said, "So somebody did take her then. This pretty much proves it."

"If it's hers, then yeah, I'd say so. Whether it is or isn't, my work doesn't change."

"Should I give it to the cops?"

"No reason not to, but I can't see what good it's going to do you. They really should have found it on their own."

We sat together, the weight of everything hovering over us. Finally Arrow broke the silence and said, "Nickel?"

"Yeah?"

"How much is it going to cost for you to help me? I don't have much; I'll do what I can to pay you."

"I don't want anything. I had a couple other things come in solid for me, so I'm flush right now."

"Thank you."

"Listen, I'm going to get out of here, do some more research. Something's sticking in my head funny. I'll talk to you soon. Page me if you need me."

She hopped off the bench, gave me a little wave, and was out of there. It was awful to see her go but nice to watch her leave. I shook my hand at Eyepatch, got the typical response, and walked to my bike. I was going to need to start wearing a jacket; it was getting cold out. A parent would probably have reminded me to do that. I rode home, my head full with hair bands, blood spots, and boot prints, as well as a dark face from my past that will never get all the way gone.

Chapter 5

My dad told me before he died to never let someone else make me be a civilian. He said that was my choice. I never believed him. Hot fires and red death taught me otherwise; Dad had been more right than I'd ever allowed myself to realize. After that, after becoming Nickel, I knew I'd never be a civilian. Work like I did for Arrow or Veronica was just practice for my future life, for my real life. Earning money was growing pot and making grown men think I was an angel on a keyboard. Could be worse; it sure had been before.

When I had been trying to figure out somewhere to stay, it had been warm out. If it had been cold, I either would have died or ended up with the state again. I made a plan, and I made it work. More dumb luck than anything, but it worked, and I didn't go back to foster care. I suppose after the fire at the Richardsons' I could have even gone to prison.

At first I wanted to leave Michigan, go somewhere else and try to start from scratch. It wasn't until I started doing research on how homeschooling worked that I realized I had a chance to live a normal life only if I stayed in Michigan. It would just take a lot of oil to keep it moving.

The house had been easy once I got my ducks in a row. I fished Craigslist for what I wanted—a nice little two-bedroom for rent with a landlord who wouldn't be too pushy as long as the checks came on time. You've got to love the Internet; I set the whole thing up via e-mail in the public library. Told him over the Web how I was a businessman who was almost never home, but my teenage son would be. He had the right reaction—he didn't care. When I told him I wanted to pay him for the first year up front, he jumped at the opportunity, barely even looked at the bum I hired to hand him a check, and even better, barely looked at me. The whole deal was over in less than ten minutes. I've got an open-ended lease that I can terminate whenever I want regardless of contract. It's hard to trace a man who doesn't exist.

That was the last time I used my real name; I put it on the fake ID I made for the bum. I still have the thing somewhere or another. My name next to a picture of a man paid two hundred bucks to take a shower and play house for a few minutes. Could an ID get any faker than that? In any case, work gets me money, and money in the mail lets me keep my place.

With that in mind, I logged back on as shyBoy. Four separate rooms just waiting for a hit. Fish on the line in minutes. I read up on a few more sex offenders by Four Oaks but felt nothing. I read the chats again and went to the one with PartyAnimal13. He wanted to private, and I said I did too. I suppose in a way I really did want to screw him.

"ASL?"

"Thirteen, male, Ohio. How about you?"

"I'm eighteen, male, Florida."

Already lying. PartyAnimal13, actually Ron Michaels of Indiana, thirty-six years old. I love computers.

"Is it hot down there?"

"It's always hot. What are you doing on here?"

"I don't know, I've just been having these urges lately. I'm not really sure what they mean, but sometimes in gym class when we're showering, I don't know, it's weird."

"I used to have feelings like that when I was your age. You know what I did? I found an older guy to help me out with my urges."

"Did it help?"

"It sure did. He just knew exactly what I wanted him to do."

"Like what?"

This is just so easy.

I strung him along for a while, let him go into the intimate details of all the awful things he wanted to do to me or any kid like me. Finally, even my strong stomach had enough and I said, "Ron, cut the crap. You've got a wife, three kids, and a dog named Rudy. Looks like a Jack Russell. Those are nice dogs, kind of wild though."

He didn't even try and explain, just bounced. I started with his work e-mail. I took a picture of the chat and sent it to him with my dummy e-mail account; the IP is blocked and makes it look like I'm out of California. The subject in the e-mail was "Ron Michaels wants to suck boys." Not my best, but it would do. While I waited for Ron to get back to me, I went back to the sex offender database. I had a brainstorm and opened another tab to look at Zappos.com.

I went right to work boots, stopped halfway typing it, and opened a tab for Amazon. Did work boots there too. I got my little notebook out, set my pager on the desk, and opened the notebook to the sketch of the boot print. My e-mail caught a ding, but

I ignored it. I opened my eyes to the world of work boots. There sure are a lot of work boots out there for a person to pick from.

After an hour I took a break from the boots and checked the e-mail. Typical.

"This is Ron, and I'm not sure what you are talking about, but I think you have someone else even though you have my personal information right. I don't see how you could think that I want to suck or molest or whatever on boys because I don't. I'm a married Christian man with a family and please leave me alone. You have the wrong guy."

All of them say this. All of them. I used to make them send me a picture of their unit before the big reveal, but it really just made for too many upset stomachs. It's one thing to know you're doing them a favor; it's another to have to see how much they appreciate it. My biggest complaint? I think most of them would get more turned on if I told them the truth about me living alone like an adult. I responded to Ron in a way I thought he'd appreciate.

"Ron, I really hate to be the bearer of bad news, but I know what you are and so do you. Look, I've got you hung up in a noose that spans continents. I'm a cop paid to do this stuff, and I don't like it any more than you do. Don't get me wrong, I think you're sick and all, but I'm not too happy with my bank account either. For a nominal sum, shipped with proof within forty-eight hours, I will change my mind about sending our talk to your boss and wife. I'll work with you as best I can, but the vehicle and house shots your wife put on her Facebook? I know you have money."

I took a break to wait. I'd come up with a few thousand matches on the boot print, from Doc Martens to Rocky, and the go-to fall tread pattern was close to what I saw in the print by the hair band. I sighed as the e-mail dinged and was happy for the distraction. There was more work to be done with the shoes than I'd anticipated, maybe a few days' worth, but money talks.

This time it was short.

"You have the wrong guy. Please leave me alone."

When I first started doing this, I actually believed guys when they'd say that. Three minutes later the same dude's user name with the exact same IP signature would pop up in the same room. I lost empathy and compassion for my fellow males that day. This was controllable, but some people took that sicko leash off on purpose. I vowed never to take it easy on one of these pervs, and it hasn't hurt my moral sensibility or wallet ever since. I like to think most of them who pay me stop. What's really scary is thinking about all of the ones that I miss. I ever tell you I don't sleep too well?

"No I don't. E-mail to your boss goes in two minutes. Your wife will get one in five. After that, it looks like Tyler and Adam have e-mail accounts, and I'm sure Leslie will too someday. I may as well shoot this their way."

I waited, got bored, and did another Google search on boot print patterns. Ron mailed me back. He was contrite, and I thought that was a reasonable enough way to be—embarrassed, but understanding his life didn't have to be destroyed. Of course he didn't know that all of my transcripts get sent to an FBI office in Detroit—just as soon as the check is cashed, of course. The hope is that they're happy enough to work with what I give them that they won't start looking for who's sending them the info. I told him two thousand, and he asked how he could know that I'd go away. I told him he didn't and that he should just hope I found a new source of income. He said he'd mail it tomorrow, and I thanked him for his haste. He didn't respond. I was hungry, and for the first time in months I went out to eat. I wanted to think, I wanted to relax, and God help me, I wanted Thai food. I put on my backpack and got on my bike. The restaurant was close, and my bike was fast; I was there in ten minutes.

The older lady working didn't recognize me, and that meant I'd waited long enough to come back. I ordered spring rolls, pad Thai, and green curry with shrimp and scallops. I ordered it all to go and sat in one of the plastic chairs they have to wait in. I learned a long time ago that you have to order at least two entrees if you don't want weird looks. If you got two, then they'd just assume you were picking up food for you and a parent. I spent the time waiting reading an issue of *People*, who, at least by the title of the magazine, were a race I understood little about. Why would anyone care who celebrities were dating? The mysteries of adults stretched far out of my realm of understanding, and I have a feeling I never will completely understand. To tell the truth, I don't mind not understanding. I paid for my order and slid the plastic bags into my backpack, hoping nothing would spill and knowing without a doubt that it most certainly would.

The weather was turning cold as I worked the pedals on my bike, and the darkness was sinking in earlier and earlier every night. My pager buzzed while I rode, and I checked it with one hand on the bars. Arrow. I stuck it back in my pocket and made a mental note to call her before I ate. The air ran through my hair; I needed to get it cut soon. Needed to mow the lawn too. So much crap to remember; it was still overwhelming even after almost two years. I walked the bike into the garage and shut it behind me.

When I got in the house, I took the backpack off at the door and set it on the floor. The smell of the food was strong, and that meant some had spilled. No sense even hoping that it wouldn't. That was like praying for the snow to stop—you'd run out of breath while it piled around you. I took the food out and put it on the table, and then I plugged in the rotary to line seven. Called Arrow. She answered on the first ring. She knew it was me.

"What took so long?"

"I was out."

"I gave the hair band to the detectives. They kept it, and the one that was at our house said they'd do some tests, but I could tell from the way he was looking at me that he thought I was being stupid." She'd been crying; I could hear it in her voice. If I was brave, I'd have invited her over for dinner. Instead I said, "Typical police. You did what you could."

"My dad still thinks she ran away, but my mom is starting to at least see the possibility that she could have been taken by somebody."

"They'll come around."

I didn't say what I was thinking: "But it'll be too late." It was probably already too late. Every second that passed, my window to find Shelby alive was closing.

"I know. It just sucks, though."

"I gotta go."

"All right. Thanks, Nic…"

I hung up the phone and unplugged it. Went to the kitchen, got out a plate and a fork. Spread rice on the plate, laid a spring roll on it. Topped the rice with green curry and put a pile of pad Thai next to it. It smelled delicious. I took it with me to the computer.

I set the food down on my desk and opened a new window. Went to Facebook, and I found Veronica's boy Jeff in about ten seconds. He was set to private, so I went to make a new profile. Gave myself the name of Amber Tease—you know, lowest common denominator and all that. Went looking for a picture for Amber on Google; typed in hot girl and went to page fifteen.

Tried again, this time with it set to safe search. Now I had something I could use. Picked a blonde at random and set it up as my avatar. Did a little more research on my girl; she had a few more pics out there, none of them obscene. She looked more college than porn star. I wrote up a short little profile for her and registered the account. Went in and added some pictures.

When my page was how I wanted it, ditsy girl 3.0, I looked up Grand Rapids, Michigan. I sent friend requests to everybody who looked like they were under twenty-five, Jeff included. I had a few dozen buddies in less than five minutes, but not Jeff. I took a break, put my feet up. I ate a spring roll, dove into the pad Thai, and tried the curry. Even getting cold, everything was fantastic. Checked my Facebook. I had a new friend—actually about a hundred more new friends, but that's okay, I have a feeling that Amber likes to party.

Jeff's account was exactly what I expected to see. Stupid pictures of a man-boy hanging out with like-minded individuals at social events. Most of the pictures were of Jeff either drunk or trying to look hard. He was better at drinking. Jeff would probably look hard for about four seconds if things ever got real around him. Relationship status listed as single. Looked like Veronica didn't know the score as well as she thought she did. I took a bite of curry, rice, sauce, and scallop. Started a message.

"What's up, hottie? Just moved here from D-Town and looking to get my drink on!!!! Anything happening this weekend I wouldn't want to miss? ;-)"

It took literally less than two minutes for this knucklehead to get back to me.

"Hey, shorty. Yeah, there's some stuff going down at the old drive-in up by Knapp Street on Friday. You need a ride?"

Lord help these kids if the cops are ever looking for them. I ate some more pad Thai and waited a second so I wouldn't sound too desperate. "I don't need a ride to the party, might need one later though. I'll see you there. XXOOXXOO ;-)"

Immediately back from Jeff: "Oh alright, you find me. I'll be by the kegs. Lookin' forwards to seein' you!"

Confirmed, then: if he was willing to try and hook up with some random girl in public, he and the girl were much less serious than Veronica had thought. Could be she was just a decent arm piece, maybe matched a couple of his shirts. I logged out and went back to my boot research. Worked at that for an hour or so and got up to put the food in the fridge. I thought about doing some more chats, but I went to bed instead.

Chapter 6

The next morning I woke up, took a shower, and ate Thai food.
Even stone cold it was terrific. I went outside and watered my garden. I was going to need to do some harvesting again soon. From looking up, it seemed a storm was coming; I had to hope it would be gone soon, or my research project on Friday would be a bust. I thought about Shelby and Arrow. That storm was already here. I went back in and put away the Thai food. Went in my room and put on my camo. I exited to the garage, got on my bike, and went back to Four Oaks.

I stopped at a gas station on the way there to grab a newspaper. The clerk gave me a look, and I stuffed some Airheads candy on top of the paper. The look went away. I walked out and tossed the candy in the garbage. I can't see a dentist, so candy is a no and twice-a-day brushing is always a must. I sat on the curb next to my bike. There was a little piece on Shelby on the front page. I scanned it, but there was no mention of a hair band. In the little picture they had she looked just like Arrow, beautiful, just smaller. I had to find that kid.

Rolling through Four Oaks, I felt something at the front of my mind, I just didn't know what. Something was sticking out and waiting to get hammered flat, but I just couldn't see it. I guess

I was so busy looking for something that I didn't see who was looking for me.

There were three of them, all on bikes that looked a lot nicer than mine, and all three of them bigger than me. Dressed nicer too, and none of them looked like they needed a haircut. I thought about my chances of just pedaling away from them and gave it up. I took my feet off the pedals and stopped the bike with my Converses. They pulled right up to me, their front wheels almost touching mine. I shifted my legs so that if I dropped the bike I could bounce free and not get hung up on the bars. The one in the middle, both in size and positioning, spoke first: "You don't live in this neighborhood."

I shook my head no, trying to make it look like I was scared. That part was easy; I had practice.

The one to my left spoke: "Then why are you here? We don't need white trash around here."

"I'm just riding my bike."

The middle one: "'I'm just widing my bwike.' You picked the wrong place to ride."

I got ready to drop the bike. This was so not what I needed right now. I needed Four Oaks to be normal, a place easy for me to move about without making waves. I kept my hands flat at my sides. If I had to get aggressive, it needed to happen fast and needed to be a surprise if I was going to have a chance. I scanned their faces. They were trying to look tough, and at least from my perspective, it was working pretty well.

The middle one said, "Got any money, trash can?"

I shook my head.

"That's going to be a problem."

The one on the right still hadn't spoken. That meant he was either the muscle or had about as much interest in this as I did.

The other two were smiling like they'd just heard the funniest joke in the world, but he had a face of stone.

The one on the left said, "We're taking that bike. Get off of it."

I dropped the bike and with the same motion pushed it forward as I hopped it up. It turned sideways, and the frame and front wheel hit their bikes, knocking their rides backwards and heads forward. Rhino says that when you hit someone, you roll your body so that your body is in the blow, not just your arm. I pushed my right fist hard into the face of the one in the middle. I felt bones shift in his nose and saw blood instantly. He kept himself busy holding his nose like he thought it might fall off. Maybe it would.

The one on the right was backing up, either to make space to attack me or to leave.

I grabbed the one on the left by the ear and started pulling down and towards me. Another rule from the gym: if you're going to put pressure on something, do it quickly. He was taller than me, and with my arm extended, my bike almost tripped me up. The kid was slapping at my wrists while I turned his ear. "You know," I said, "it only takes about five pounds of pressure for me to tear this ear off of your head. Do you want to spend the rest of your life turning your head to have a conversation?"

I gave the kid with the nose a look. He was just staring at the pavement under his feet, though, and the kid from the right was gone.

I let go of the ear, and he grabbed at it to make sure I hadn't taken a souvenir. I said, "Go home." He rubbed the ear a couple of times, and I could see he was near to crying. Stupid bullies, hunting in packs only made you safer if you beat up on kids who wouldn't fight back.

I turned back to the kid with the bloody nose. He let go of the nose, clenched his fists, and dropped the bike. Internally I sighed, listening to Rhino talk in his thick accent: "Throw upper-cuts from your waist; turn when you hit." Externally I turned that nose from a bike ramp to a ski lift. He actually fell down to cry. Don't get me wrong, I'm no hero, but kids today, they've got no stones. I left him lying on the pavement while Lefty just stared at him. I went back to my bridge. Things had changed.

I laid the bike on the guardrail and walked on down to troubled turf. Before there had been a hair band and a purpose, but now there was the thought that maybe the abductor had been back. No such luck. Looking over the guardrail it was apparent that I'd expected too much out of my town. Instead of one boot print, there were about a thousand waffle-print cop shoe prints, and trust me, after the last few days, I knew shoes. Stupid bastards. I walked to the creek and back. Any clues they hadn't taken they'd run over.

I hauled the bike up and rode home. I still had that iron taste in my mouth of being almost there, but I pushed it aside. Almost there could wait, and hopefully Shelby could too. I rode home. Definitely sweatshirt weather, and the fact that the sun was slowly leaving the sky didn't help much either. I swear it gets colder by the day, if not by the hour. I parked the bike in the garage and pulled it right back out—I'd forgotten the post office. I rode into the black.

Chapter 7

The post office, like most public buildings, undergoes a change after nightfall. For the post office that means creeps and aliens, guys who look like us but are as at home with us normals as we are with our pets. They dog that line of civilian and participant, and we watch as they feast or flounder. Most of the time they flounder, occasionally ascend a clock tower and make war on people who can't fight back. If that's success, I don't want it. I'll take living over that. I'll take anything.

It was cold and dark but not empty. If there's a creepy building to be in, it's a post office after hours. The building is wall-to-wall weirdoes. I don't know if it's a planned thing or not, but they built it, so they come. Usually I avoid this scene as much as possible, but when I'm working a case it gets tough. Missing one day wasn't the end of the world, but it sure made me stressed. This was the closest I got to public, and it never was comfortable.

I ride solo, by choice and by measure; I make myself as available as the world requests. Unfortunately, I also have to make a buck. I parked my bike in the rack and took a deep breath to steel myself. It didn't work, so I tried again. No good. I left the bike and went inside.

The lights they run at night aren't the same ones they have on during the day. They aren't quite emergency lights, like in a hospital or a school, but they're not much better. They make for long shadows. The merchandise—the boxes and knock-off bean-bag toys—was all locked up. Really the only thing the building was good for was mailing a letter, buying stamps, and checking a post office box.

I crossed the tile floor, my feet making loud clicks as I went. There were a couple of ghouls doing the same thing I was; they needed a secret place to get mail, secrets important enough to them to bear them privately. I moved past a man in a flannel shirt, and he offered me a wide grin. I gave nothing back. My usual show of acting like it was normal for a kid like me to be in the post office at night was broken; I wouldn't have fooled a blind man. I was rattled. Maybe it was the fight in the afternoon, maybe it was Shelby. Whatever it was, I wasn't right. I unlocked my box and took the lone envelope. No return address. I folded it and pushed it into my pocket next to my pager. I walked out as quickly as I could and took the chain off of my bike.

The freak from inside was waiting on me in a truck with the windows rolled down. He snaked his head out of the passenger window and said, "What are you doing out so late?"

"Checking my dad's mail for him. He's laid up right now."

I'd established myself: there was a parent, and I would be missed.

"You need a ride? You can throw your bike in the truck."

"No, I live close. Thanks though."

I would be missed soon.

"Alright."

He backed out, and I felt relieved—he was going the opposite way. I rolled out of the parking lot, my heart thudding in my chest. Then the wind carried the noise of a truck behind me. Crap. I gave a look over my shoulder—same truck, with the headlights off. I passed over a small hill, the truck quieted, and I started moving as fast as I could, using the back side of the hill to carry my momentum.

I steered myself down the first road I came to, took a quick right turn, and drove up the driveway of a black house. They had a stack of cut wood on the side of the house, and I dove behind it. I let my bike lay in front of the wood in a spot where there was no light. The truck drove by, circled back, and disappeared. I picked up the bike and rode home.

My hands shook on the grips, and my breath was weak. I had research to do, but it wasn't in me. I parked the bike and went inside. I didn't even check the envelope; I just sat on the couch. That's where I woke in the morning, fully dressed, fists clenched. I'd missed three pages in the night. The first one was from Gary— the others would have to wait.

Chapter 8

I plugged in line one and called Gary. He answered on the third ring. "Nickel?"

Gary knew better than that. "Not on this line."

"Can you call my cell?"

"Sure. When?"

"Now. I need to talk now."

Crap. "All right. Give me a half hour."

I hung up the phone and looked at the pager to see who else had decided to brighten my day. Arrow and a number I didn't recognize. They'd have to wait. I ate some crackers and went to the garage; a shower and new clothes would have to wait too. I reevaluated and went back inside, brushed my teeth, came back out, got on the bike, and got going. I was at the gas station in ten minutes.

I gave a quick look around. There were a couple of civilians getting gas and a bored-looking black girl reading some magazine in the little booth. Nobody seemed the least bit interested in the kid with the disheveled clothes who needed a shower. I dropped a quarter in and called Gary.

"Nic..."

"Knock it off."

He was flustered. Gary was never flustered. I was starting to feel a little penned in myself.

"Sorry. I'm stressed."

"What's going on?"

"I almost got caught."

"How?"

"A kid I sell to got busted and rolled on me…he only had a half ounce, and he rolled on me. Can you believe that?"

I could, point of fact. I had no problem believing it at all. "Were you holding?"

"No, but I've got almost two ounces at home. They searched my locker. The principal was going to call the cops!"

"Anything in your car?"

"No. I did everything you said to do."

"Where's your supply?"

"In the woods. Like I said, I did everything you said to do."

"Good, that's good."

"It's not good, dude. I need money! Seriously, I extended myself pretty far on my last buy, and I need to make a car payment."

"That's sloppy."

"Look, I know that, okay? I screwed up, but at least I didn't screw up big-time. I just can't sell for a little bit. I got to let this heat die a little."

"Your principal didn't believe you?"

"He didn't believe a word I had to say. He was looking at me like he wanted to eat me, and when they searched my locker and didn't find anything, he got pissed, dude, like seriously angry. He's going to be out for me for a while."

Not good.

"How much time you going to take off?"

"I'm not sure."

"Anybody else you trust?"

"Like, *trust* trust? No."

"You sure? Think hard."

"Look, Nic…I don't need to think hard, alright? The friends I have, I have them because of money and because of weed. They know it, and I know it. I'm even okay with it, but not one of those kids would be worth a thing to me in a storm. You're the only real friend I've ever had, and we've never even met."

I didn't think it would be appropriate to remind him that the only bonds we had were weed and money too.

"Take a month off, no more, no less. If the heat's not off by then, we'll need to reevaluate whether a sales position is still viable for you. I'll throw fifteen hundred in the box tonight; grab it in the morning. Will that settle you for a month?"

"That would be amazing, dude. You'd really do that?"

"No problem. Get things squared up, get your stash back, and get selling. We'll need to make up lost ground, but that's okay."

"Thanks, man."

I hung up, breathing hard. Was Gary rolling over on me? Could he connect to me if he tried hard enough? The answer to the first was no, and to the second? I didn't want to think about that, not even on a nice day with the sun on my face. I gave another look around the gas station and went home. I pedaled slowly, like I didn't have a care in the world. I was worried about Gary; even the thought of him faltering made my world go gray. He'd taken time and energy to set up, and I'm not sure I had the time or energy to do it again. I parked the bike and went inside. I thought about lunch and took a shower.

When I got out, I dried off and dressed. I ate a PB&J and went outside, turned on the water, and sat on the stoop. I thought about Gary and pushed the thought away. I needed to worry about Shelby. I remembered I had phone calls to make. Looking at the garden, I could see some work that needed doing outside. I went in to call Arrow; I could harvest pot later.

I called her on the two line. I couldn't remember if I'd called her on that number before or not. She said, "Hello?"

"It's me."

"I need to talk."

"You want to meet at the park?"

"Sure. Same time?"

"That's good for me."

She hung up. My type of girl, a fast learner. I looked at the pager and called the other number I'd missed while I was sleeping. No answer, no machine. I hoped it wasn't too important. I went in the garage and got my gardening supplies and a bucket. The rest of the afternoon was spent trimming pot and carrying it to the basement to dry. I was going to have a storage issue if Gary didn't get his poop in a group with a quickness. When I was done working, I needed another shower. I felt like I'd been climbing pine trees, and I smelled like I was trying to relive the sixties all by myself. It was time to go, so I left.

Chapter 9

Arrow was waiting for me when I got to the bench. Eyepatch was right where he was supposed to be, and everything looked good. I left my bike at the rack and walked over to her. She was wearing a little skirt and a short-sleeved hoodie. If she was trying to look incognito, it wasn't working. Come to think of it, I'm not sure if a girl who looked like that could go incognito. I sat next to her, and she said, "Any luck?"

"I almost got my butt kicked in Four Oaks yesterday."

She pulled air in through her teeth. "Tommy Van Andel?"

"I didn't get a name." I didn't mention that I had almost gotten an ear.

"Yeah, it was Tommy. I was wondering how he got the cast on his nose."

"Parting gift."

"I bet he's sorry he ran into you."

"So I did good."

"He's a little punk; he had it coming."

"He pretty much mailed me a letter and asked me to do it."

"Why were you in Four Oaks?"

"I was just looking around, trying to get a focus on who would be in a good position to take your sister."

"And?"

"My line of thinking was upset by your neighborhood thugs."

She grimaced. "Sorry, I should have said something. It was the last thing on my mind."

"It's alright. They know better for next time."

"You never know. Tommy's not a fast learner."

"I can just teach him twice. I don't mind."

I gave her a smile; she gave me a weak one back.

"The cops found one of Shelby's shoes," she said.

"Where?"

"In the woods by the bridge."

"Will you take me there?"

"Of course."

She stood and smoothed the skirt down her legs like it was the most natural thing in the world; I did my best to catch all of it. When I waved as we walked by Eyepatch, Arrow gave me a look and did the same. I hoped she might get a reaction, but nothing happened. Bummer. I got the bike, unwrapping the chain in front of her—letting her see a secret, even if just a small one. I pedaled, she walked, and we were there in less than ten minutes.

I dismounted at the bridge and did the same show of wrapping the bike to look like it was locked. To her credit, Arrow didn't ask why. She held out a hand after she hopped over the ledge, and she held onto it as I jumped the guardrail and then continued to as we slid down together. When we hit bottom, she finally let go and darn near broke my heart. I vowed to never wash it again.

We went to the stream. "There's where I found the hair band," I said. "Right next to it was a big boot print. I did some work on that, but it was a common tread, nothing there. So how far down did they say they found the shoe?"

She led me along the water, the light peeking in through the trees. It was beautiful, and I was also pretty sure it was where an eleven-year-old girl had been taken and possibly killed. It kind of wrecked all that natural beauty, to be honest with you. We stopped after about a five-minute walk when we hit the police tape. There were footprints everywhere, both dog and people. It was immediately apparent they'd brought an army back here. Any evidence they missed was destroyed tenfold.

I walked over to the tape and tried to look busy, but when I turned to Arrow, she had her arms folded and I could tell my Sam Spade impersonation held no water. "How far do these woods go?" I asked her.

"If we keep at it, we'll find ourselves on blacktop in about five minutes. If we go back the way we came, it'll be a lot longer."

"If he took your sister, could he have come in this way and then walked through the woods out to the road?"

"I guess."

"Will you take me there?"

"Let's go."

We didn't talk while we moved, just walked at an honest pace by the water and next to the trees. There had been a lot of foot traffic recently, and the soft earth at the edge of the creek bore the abuse of all the shoes. Cop prints were everywhere. I kept my eyes and ears open. I was looking for anything, but all I saw was flora and Arrow. Natural beauty in both cases. I could hear the road before we got there, and I followed Arrow up an incline to a bridge not unlike the one I'd parked my bike on. We watched a Dodge van pass in front of us, and then we walked onto the road.

It wasn't much to look at. The difference was that this road didn't act as an inlet to a neighborhood. This was country enough to have some time to stop—with a little luck, time enough to throw a girl into a van. For the first time, it occurred to me that Shelby could have been taken by a pair. It would have made the work even easier to have one of them in the woods, the other waiting in a van or pretending to change a flat. I figured what they did, if it was a pair of them, was lure Shelby into the woods and then drugged her. From there whoever did it could carry her through the woods and to a waiting vehicle. It would have been easy. I shuddered and looked back into the woods. I could see it all running over and over in my head, like a little newsreel.

Arrow dragged me out of it, sounding like the young girl she was for the first time since I'd met her. "Nickel," she said, "we need to find her."

Her eyes were wet, and I stuck a matchstick in my teeth. Things were coming together for me, slowly but surely. There was something here, and I just needed to get my guts all the way through it. I needed time, and it was at a premium; I'd spent too much time not finding Shelby already. Still, there was nothing I could think to do right now but turn to Arrow, let the matchstick dance in my mouth a little bit, and ask, "Want to get some dinner?"

Chapter 10

I took her to a place I'd always wanted to go but never had, Graydon's Crossing, a little English pub about equidistant from our houses. We'd stopped by her house to pick up her bike, and she chained hers the same way I did outside of the restaurant. Maybe I was coming off kind of cool. (A guy could hope.) I held the door to let her in and followed after her. I thought I'd made a mistake at first; it was more of a bar than a restaurant, and I thought we might get bounced before the door closed behind us. Instead, a waitress came and led us to a booth with high backs. Aside from the opening to get in, it was quite private. I ordered a water, and Arrow got a Diet Coke.

The menu was thick like a book, and I settled on a rare rib eye and potatoes. I hadn't had a steak in forever. I was okay on the little gas grill out back of the house, but I couldn't cook steak to save my life. Arrow ordered the same. God bless a woman who loves red meat. We put the order in with the waitress and sat there, taking it all in. I couldn't speak for her, but I didn't feel like all that much of a kid for once in my life—I was a guy working a job for a dame. If that's not a good feeling, then I don't think I know what is.

She said, "Have you been here before?"

"No, but I've ridden past it about a million times and always wanted a reason to come here."

"I'm a reason?"

She was smiling, and I said, "You're a good reason."

She looked me in the eyes, and I could feel the fire in my cheeks before she even spoke.

"Nickel, you're not like any kid I ever met in my life."

I did my best to mentally chase the redness from my face. She was right, but I didn't say anything. I might be young, small for my age, and way over my head with the girl across from me, but even I know not to argue with a compliment that awesome.

"Do you go to school?"

"No."

"Did you ever?"

"I've gone enough to know that they can't teach me anything I can't learn on my own."

"You heard that in a movie."

I smiled. I probably had, I just couldn't remember which one. I changed the subject. "How are your parents doing?"

"Not good. My dad still has this idea in his head that she ran away and everything's his fault. My mom just sits in her room and cries all day; I think she's been drinking again. She used to when I was little, and I've always been scared she might start back up. Shelby went missing, and we're falling apart without her."

"We need to find her."

She reached out and took my hand and rubbed my palm with her fingers; she had on lime green nail polish. "Thank you for helping me, Nickel."

She smiled, but her eyes were welling with tears. If there was a moment where we were more just than two kids looking for a lost girl, that was it. I was trying to think of something good to say

49

when our food came. The steak looked good, but it was terrible timing. Arrow wiped her eyes with her napkin and took up her knife and fork. She said, "Let's eat."

And that's what we did. My steak was delicious, just the right amount of fat to keep the meat from drying out. The potatoes were good too, but I can make a potato at home. Arrow must have agreed with me because she was eating at the same pace as me and saying as much as I was about it.

When I had eaten enough to make me feel like I might explode, I put my knife and fork down. Arrow didn't. She cleaned that plate until the only thing left was ceramic, and then she wiped her face primly and said, "That was really good."

"Agreed."

"So what was it you had to ask me?"

"I need a favor."

"You need a favor? I already told you I don't have much money."

"It's not that kind of favor. I'm working another job right now, and I could use some help."

"You think I could help you? How?"

"I'm watching a kid for another client; she thinks he's falling in with the wrong crowd. I got myself invited to a party tonight, and if I went with you, I wouldn't look so out of place. I really just need to figure out what his kick is so his mom can sleep better at night."

"Alright."

"You'll do it? That was easier than I thought."

"Sure, why not? Nickel?"

"Yeah?"

"How'd you get yourself invited to a party that you don't know anyone at?"

I told her about the Facebook hustle, and she smiled and laughed a little bit at the end.

"In any case, the whole thing will go easier with a pretty girl around me. The guys won't notice so quickly that I'm a foot and a half shorter than everybody else."

"You really think so?"

"Are you kidding? Guys are knuckleheads."

She blushed. "Not that. About me being pretty."

I gave her my best tough guy look and said, "Arrow, I know so."

She smiled back at me, and if I had died right then it would've been just fine by me. The waitress dropped off our tab, and I took it before Arrow had even seen it was there to be taken. She gave me a look, and I gave her one back.

"My idea, I pay."

She got a look like she knew that's how it would be. I stuffed money in the little book they give you with a bill in decent restaurants and said, "Let's go."

Back at our bikes, unwrapping the chains, Arrow asked, "What's the plan?"

"I'm going to go home and get ready. You go get yourself prepped—think party—and ride your bike to the gas station just outside of Four Oaks, the Mobil. I'll pick you up from there at seven."

"You have a car?"

"A cab."

"Oh, right."

She mounted her bike and I mounted mine, and we were off. It wasn't a date, I had to tell myself over and over again, but it had been nice to have a real talk with someone, to take off that veneer and just be a kid. Deep down, I'm just a survivor, and that survivor has his own special set of rules. Sometimes, like tonight, that veneer slips a little, and I get to be normal. That little voice always wins, but tonight I got to have dinner with a pretty girl. If I'm smiling, it's not part of the act.

Chapter 11

I put the bike in the garage and closed the door behind me with the button on the wall. Walked in the house and stripped down as I moved. Threw my shirt and pants in the hamper, and they both fell off and onto the floor. I really did need to do some laundry. Ignoring the mess as best I was able, I got to work on finding some new duds. A pair of ripped jeans for the legs and a Dickies T-shirt. Weather crossed my mind, and I grabbed a plain black hoodie. Once everything was assembled on the bed, I just stood there looking stupid for a few seconds, thinking. I had no idea what I was getting into, so I had to be ready for anything.

I stuck my hand under the bed and pulled out my disaster box. It was really just an under-bed storage container, but what it held for me couldn't have been much more important. That box could let me leave right now, no questions asked, if I had to. I never questioned whether or not I could do it; I needed to remember that if I had to, I would. I pulled the white top off of the black box and looked over my kit.

I always keep ten grand in the box, nine thousand in hundreds and the last G in smaller denominations. The money has been ironed and is stored in moisture-proof sealed bags. I have a nine-hundred-thousand-volt taser that I bought illegally on eBay, two huge cans of mace labeled for Michigan as bear spray, and a K-Bar survival knife. In addition to the large cans of bear spray, I also have a pen that works correctly and also contains a few milliliters of mace if you depress the button just right. I've got a night vision monocular, a pair of high-end binoculars, and a spotting scope with a little tripod—pretty much everything for your long-distance observer.

About a year or so ago I got hired to find a lost cat—not a big deal until I found out it had been consumed in a Chinese restaurant I won't name. I got paid to burn the joint down, and I did it with a smile on my face. Call me a hypocrite for wanting to eat meat but not liking to hear a cat got eaten, but that's where I draw the line. I have a few boxes of those strike anywhere matches that you can only get in army surplus stores in my box as well. I usually keep a couple in my pocket; they're nice to chew on. With the matches there are a couple of tins of butane and propane, handy little accelerants if the need arises.

The last section of the box was the least savory. No one would mistake my K-Bar or taser for being a tool to say hello in some new way, but the rest of this stuff was just nasty. Handcuffs, leg cuffs, a ball gag. A weighted hat and gloves, a plastic knife that was as sharp as steel and could pass through any metal detector. A flare gun with an incendiary charge, two starter pistols, a wrist rocket that really would work at about five feet or so—it wasn't the best arsenal, but it was all mine.

The whole mess rounds off with a ghillie suit—it's green and covered in loose strips of shaggy green, brown, and black camouflage, like a sniper would wear to really disappear—two strings of M-80s, a tin of gunpowder, a can of beer that will shoot white phosphorous if opened—it has a twin in the fridge—a pair of knuckle dusters made of polymer, custom-made steel toe-guards that hook into any pair of All-Stars. Last but not least, a hand grenade with about thirty rounds of .50 caliber machine gun ammo taped around it. I call that my "get out of jail free card." A similar piece was built to fit in my bike's frame and work by a ten-mile remote. I like it in the garage, fear it below my crotch, and don't think it will ever get installed.

I pulled the clothes on, laced my shoes up, and grabbed the mace pen, a starting pistol, and almost the night vision. I had a sidekick—no need to be on the outside. I might not be Amber Tease, but I can still play a role. I went down to the basement and grabbed a half ounce of pot. Rolling it just as well as I could, I spun up ten of the biggest joints this town is ever going to see. I dropped those in a scent-lock hunting bag and called Lou. He was there in ten minutes.

We're a good combo. I don't want to talk, and neither does he.

Lou asked where we were going, and I told him, putting the gas station first. If he had thoughts on the matter, he kept quiet. He'd never cared before, and this time was no different. We slid into that Mobil like the cab was slicked in Moly Grease. Arrow showed in the window, and I opened the door. She looked how I hoped she would, easy access and low morals. Short skirt, low top, all a parody of Arrow except the attitude. She let me get a peek, winked, and shook a finger, and then she zipped her sweatshirt. The girl wasn't a tease, she was a blade. She got in the car and had the sense not to talk. Lou drove, we sat.

Chapter 12

We were to Knapp in no time. I made Lou drive us a quarter mile south and drop us off. I flipped him fifty—the ride was twenty, five was for the tip, and the rest was for next time. I paid for next time every time. Lou would drive me to Cali if I asked, no questions. I'm pretty sure I've already paid for the trip in full, too. We slipped out of the cab, and I said, "Two hours, right here."

Lou nodded, Arrow crooked out an elbow, and we walked to our party.

You could hear it at the same time that light from the bonfires became visible. I could tell from the parked cars that there were a lot of people there, but the oppressive noise of the rap coming from the stereos made it tough to know how many people were actually attending. I let go of Arrow's arm, which was about the last thing in the world I wanted to do, but unfortunately, the looks we would get as a couple would be dangerous. I was better off as a little brother or a neighbor she felt sorry for. I was just glad she was from a different school district. She might know a couple of people here, but she wouldn't know many—all the better to stay under the radar.

The music got louder the closer we got, and I could see the numbers. There were hundreds of kids here. I knew that it was going to be big, but this was a serious party. A very drunk high school kid walked past us as we approached and muttered something unintelligible. I'm pretty sure he said hello. The closer we got the more obvious it became that not only was there a party, but something more primal was going on; there was a great circle of them built around some event. We passed the kegs and a fresh pile of vomit and approached the circle. Space was made for us without our asking—thank goodness I brought Arrow. I didn't know what to make of it. Whoever heard of a party where the kegs weren't the stars of the show? The crowd screamed and made enough space around the circle for us to move in.

It looked like the kegs weren't going to be ignored all night. This part of the show was over. I could see a form lying still in what had been the center of the storm. Two other forms stood over the one lying there, and finally, after talking between themselves, they lifted him off of the ground. He stood on shaky legs, wobbled twice, and righted himself. They walked right past Arrow and me. The kid had taken a horrible beating. Blood came off of his face in a river that looked black in the firelight. Small bruises contorted his head. He looked more like a squash than a high school kid; I just hoped he wasn't Jeff. We watched him disappear into the crowd, and Arrow and I did our best to assimilate into it as well.

Guys were looking her up and down, and some of the girls were too, but it was working because they were ignoring the short kid who'd come with her. I reached into my pocket, wriggled for a second, and made a joint appear from the scent-lock bag. I passed it to Arrow from my fist to hers, and she gave me a look. She knew what it was, and that was a start. I just hoped she didn't smoke the stuff. The last thing I needed was for her to forget why we were here. An older kid approached us—he wasn't Jeff, that would have been way too convenient, but he was a monster. He had the rippling arms and tight chest of a weight lifter, and the chicken legs and thick waist to prove he didn't know what he was doing in the gym. Arrow met his eyes with hers and said, "Hi."

"Hey girl, where you from?"

"I live in Four Oaks, but my cousin goes to Forest Hills."

"That's why I don't recognize you."

His eyes scoped her up and down, making a show of it. "You look good."

"I know."

Arrow, girl of my dreams.

"Who's the kid?"

"My little brother."

"Mom got out the ugly stick for him."

She rubbed my head. "He's kind of cute. You smoke?"

"You mean weed?"

She rolled her eyes at him.

"Of course." Arrow produced the joint and rolled it between two fingers. I took a match from my pocket, lit it on my belt buckle, and held it for her cupped in my hands. She lit the thing, exhaled swiftly, and passed it to him. Our activity—well, and the fact that it involved Arrow smoking—was earning a small crowd. I slipped Arrow two more. We were getting good at that; we would have been perfect in a crooked card game. She made them disappear into the pocket of her hoodie. The joint came back, and Arrow faked hitting it, pulling the smoke into her mouth but then easing it out under her arm as she passed the J to an older high school girl who might have been beautiful if I wasn't in love. The girl looked at Arrow and decided she was worth talking to. She said, "Thanks."

The word was followed by rough coughing. My hard work in the garden was paying off, now more than just in my wallet. The girl looked glazed already. Arrow turned to her and said, "Do you know Jeff?"

The girl turned her head on a swivel that looked broken. I knew I grew good stuff, but I'd never actually seen somebody use it. It looked like about as much fun as riding my bike in the fog. She spoke, slow and deliberate, each word a sentence.

"You mean Jeff Rogers?"

"Yes."

"He's so cool. He's fighting tonight."

"He's going to be in a fight?"

"Yeah, he's got a fight against some big black dude from downtown. Jeff's a total badass, but I heard the black guy is too."

"Is that what this is all about, fights?"

"For sure, that and getting wasted."

I was learning a lot about Jeff already. My pot was working like truth serum. We were building up a crowd. Arrow produced the other joints, and I came up with a match. Flame met green, and eager faces lit up in the night with quality orthodontics. Arrow distributed the goods. I felt like some kind of weed messiah, a prophet whose followers had found him in the holy land. I made two more appear in Arrow's hand. At least so far, this was going just as easy as could be. I watched the big kids smoke pot that the pretty girl they didn't know passed around. If I'd been of a mind to, I could have poisoned the lot of them.

The music since we'd walked up had been rap, thumping bass while feeble-minded individuals talked about living hard in million-dollar mansions. If they'd ever been real street, that grease had come off a long time ago. When the music changed, soulful now, old-school R&B, I knew it was starting. Pushed like surfers on a monster wave, we moved with the crowd. Arrow and I stayed at the front, the sweet smoke of my gardening project making the air seem tighter around us. The pit where they fought was sand; I hadn't noticed that before, but I could see it now. Sand is hard to fight in; you can't move your feet like in a ring or on solid ground.

I saw him as he walked up. Had to be Jeff's opponent. The kid was huge, with muscles in so many places that he looked like a caricature. He was flanked by two guys who could have been behemoths in their own right but looked small next to him. The crowd parted to let them pass, and when he reached the edge of the sand, he took his shirt off. There wasn't an ounce of fat on him that I could see. If Jeff wasn't good, he was going to get himself killed. The kid paced the ring, looking like an African nightmare. He came back to where he'd entered and just stood there waiting. He flexed his hands, and I could hear the knuckles crack over the din of the music and the crowd. The music was quieter now, and I could hear a collective gasp. Their hero was coming.

It was an odd thing to listen to the crowd and music. Drunken teenagers were screaming for blood while the slow bass of the R&B kicked over them. Grooving and shouting mixed together with the sweet smell from Arrow and the reek of beer in the wind. Love and hate squashed in together. The crowd parted like rats on a sinking ship, and I saw Jeff.

He was already shirtless, well muscled but not overbuilt, constructed for time and speed, not muscles just for the sake of muscles. I watched him walk in alone, no handlers or friends to go with him. I gave the black kid a look. If he was impressed by Jeff, it wasn't showing. The crowd was catcalling, yelling for their hero to spill blood, crying for death. Angry words from the mouths of babes. I plucked a match out of my pocket and lit it, and Arrow got the pot moving. I looked to the sand pit as the pretty girl I'd brought to the party got even more popular. If there was a referee, I couldn't see him.

Jeff bounded around the sand pit like he'd just been loosed from a trap, bits of earth flying up from his feet, and when he passed in front of us, I could see that his hands were wrapped. The anticipation was building in the crowd. I could feel them growing together, swelling and ready to see a war—like I imagine Roman spectators looked when the handlers released the lions. A skinny little Hispanic kid I hadn't seen came to the middle of the sand pit. They were reverent for him—aside from some coughing, a product of my pot I'm sure, there was total silence. He spoke.

"Tonight our main event, Jeff 'The Executioner' Rogers and Dewayne Walters. Gentlemen, are you ready?"

Both of them nodded, short little flickers of their chins. Someone tried to pass me a joint, and I shook my head. I'd come to see what the kid's trip was, and now I wanted to see a fight. I was as ready for blood as the crowd was. I looked at Arrow; I could see she felt the same way.

Chapter 13

Jeff moved first, circling away from where he'd started. He had good footwork, nothing he'd learned on his own. I didn't know about what else he had, but the kid moved like a boxer. Dewayne just eyed him like he'd seen a man dance before and wasn't all that impressed by it then either.

Someone catcalled, "Kill him, Jeff!"

The crowd roared approval. Jeff flicked a jab twice and waded into striking distance. If Dewayne was scared, he didn't show it; he just threw those big arms up and whistled one down the pipe on Jeff. Jeff took half of the punch on his forearm and ducked his head to miss the rest. Dewayne followed it with a sloppy hook. The jab was supposed to have hurt Jeff; the hook was meant to kill him. Before that hook had even left Dewayne's shoulder, Jeff had hit the bigger kid with two hard body shots, and Dewayne staggered, throwing another hook. Jeff bounced away, came back in, and peppered Dewayne with three shots. I could hear them from where I stood, even over the crowd: two to Dewayne's head, another hard shot to his body, all three with a sound like a man slapping a steak onto a counter.

If the blows hurt Dewayne, he didn't show it. He lumbered off three punches of his own and came close on the second, a hard cross that Jeff was forced to eat on his arms. He responded in kind, attacking his larger opponent with a spray of shots that peppered him. Dewayne staggered after a crushing right, and the crowd screamed for their hero. I thought it was over then, that Jeff had won. I was wrong. The fight was just starting.

Dwayne may have looked hurt, but he wasn't. Jeff was coming in for the kill as the big man bounced back and threw a straight right hand into Jeff's breadbasket. Now they were both hurt. Jeff lowered an arm and staggered back. Dewayne's corner was screaming for their fighter. Jeff managed to shuck and roll through the next few shots Dewayne fired at him, but the last shot in a four-strike combo connected hard. As Jeff bounced away, I could see the start of a nasty cut under his left eye.

Now it was Jeff's turn. The punch to his midsection had hurt him badly, but the one to his face had woken him up. He came at Dewayne hard, winging punches that were meant to make his opponent cover up. Dewayne did, burying his face between his two massive arms, and Jeff grabbed the back of his head and leapt into the air, his momentum stopped when his knee crashed into Dewayne's face. They froze like that for a second, and then Jeff's feet were flat in the sand again. He leapt again, and another knee exploded on Dewayne's face; I was shocked he was still standing. Jeff was smiling, grinning at all of us as he leapt for the last time. The last knee actually popped Dewayne's head up from the shell he was ineffectively hiding in. Jeff let go, and the big man fell face-first to the sand. The fight couldn't have been any more over if Jeff had shot Dewayne in the face. The sand around Dewayne's face was black with blood as his friends helped him to his feet.

Jeff waited until the other man had stood. The crowd was already dispersing around Arrow and me. In the sand pit, Jeff shook hands with the man he'd bested, and Dewayne and his friends walked off to see about some repairs. I could see his nose canted at an angle it hadn't been before. I looked at Arrow and found her staring at Jeff the way a starving man on an island would at a plate of ribs. I poked her in the side with my elbow. She looked down at me, the trance broken.

"Let's go," I said. "Lou will be ready for us soon."

"Don't you have to meet Jeff?"

"No. I'll see him tomorrow."

"Can I come?"

"I'll think about it."

Inside I felt an odd turmoil. This was mission accomplished, assuming Rhino would play along. Yet, Arrow liked Jeff—I could see it all over her face, and there was nothing I could do about it. We'd been to dinner just a few hours ago, and we'd connected— maybe just a little, but we had connected. It was a fight I could see no way of winning.

We slunk away from the party pit as carefully as we'd come. A lot of people were dispersing now that their bloodlust had been sated. I had an idea up my sleeve for Jeff. The problem had turned out to be entirely different than I had expected. It would take a bit of finagling, but nothing I couldn't handle. Arrow and I didn't talk on the way back to the cab. I was thinking and so was she, and I was glad I didn't know the details of what she was thinking about—it was hard enough knowing the general drift.

Lou was right where I'd asked him to be. We piled in, and I told him to take us back to where we'd picked up Arrow. Lou grunted—I think it might have been the most he'd ever said to me. Arrow and I sat across the cab from each other. When were about halfway to the gas station, I gave her a look; she gave me one back, but it wasn't all there. She was thinking about Jeff. We dropped her off, and I went home. I paid Lou and told him I'd be in touch. He rolled up the window and left. I went in the house and went to bed. I had a dream about a man hovering in the sky like he was flying.

Chapter 14

When I went to water the plants the next morning, more were ready for harvest. I pushed the thought aside and tried to push aside my dream. That one was poking at the back of my head like an ice pick, though.

I jumped on Amber's Facebook account and messaged Jeff. "Hey sweetie, I saw you at the party, but you had so many people around you I felt shy! I'm NEVER a shy girl. I don't know what came over me. Will you meet me at the same place this afternoon so I can tell you I'm sorry?"

If that didn't work, nothing would. Got a message back; we were meeting at two. I had some work to do. I ate some eggs, the last in the carton, and hopped in the shower. It was Saturday, no camo necessary. I threw on a Hot Water Music shirt and jeans. Even when I get to pick, my clothes aren't very exciting. I found the pot, starter pistol, and pepper spray pen in my pockets from the night before. I put them all back in the box, grabbed some money, and went out to my bike. I had a fleeting thought of calling Arrow but decided not to. I could always use a pay phone later if I changed my mind. I pedaled off into the world; I had to make a stop before I got my face-to-face with Jeff.

I wheeled over and got ready for some real bike riding. Where I was going wasn't far enough in my mind to justify calling Lou, but it was close.

I hadn't seen Rhino in almost a month. He owns a jiu-jitsu gym over on the west side of town, and I was a twice-a-dayer there for a little bit. Rhino came up on his own dime when he was little, all the way from Brazil. He told me once that he started to learn jiu-jitsu so he could teach his stepfather a lesson. The lesson was hard enough that he had to go out of the country. Rhino never told me how he got to where he was today, but there were pictures around the gym, old guys with a very young Rhino, that spoke a mouthful. There were just as many pictures of Rhino with young kids, kids who had a light in their eyes. If Rhino met a sex offender, the guy would be lucky if all he did was die.

I heard, and again, Rhino just won't talk about this stuff, that Rhino runs a special class sometimes. Shows kids how to fight adults. Shows them how to pull off an ear or blind you with a remote control or break a nose with one shot, maybe even how to tear stuff off of somebody. You know, the real wet work. It's possible I went to a class like that, but I'm like Rhino, I don't talk about that business.

When I got there, I parked my bike in the bike rack, no chain. At Rhino's the word was different: your bike would get tore up if you locked it to the rack. There was no theft there.

I walked in. There was no bell over the door, but there were two plastic seats by it. I knew the game, so I sat down. I sat and watched guys roll on their lunch break. There were a couple who were good, a few who weren't, and one guy giving the instructors fits—he looked like he might have been the one teaching them. It was a decent bunch for the lunch break. Rhino was off to the side, talking to one of his teachers and lauding the student who had almost buried his teacher in a triangle choke, a move where you force your opponent's head into your crotch over their arm. You pull the arm and duck your legs, and they go to bed. Classic Brazil; I'm sure the original involved a knife.

Rhino looked over my way. I gave him a nod, and he nodded back. He tapped the instructor by him on the shoulder and pointed at me. I was either going to get bounced in a bad way or get to talk to my teacher. The instructor was wearing a gi, and he circled the outside of the cage and the ring, looped at the mats, and finally stopped in front of me. He said, "You need to speak?"

"I do." He held a hand up and snapped. I could hear Rhino nod, I could feel it. The instructor he'd sent extended his arm and pointed ahead of him to the floor. He said, "After you."

I nodded like I was supposed to and got walking around the facility. Rhino's eyes had me on lockdown the whole way. They weren't mean, and they weren't nice. They were even. I felt like twin lasers were pinching into my shirt. Rhino has that way with everyone. If there is a better friend to troubled children, I've yet to meet him. I walked up to Rhino, and he gave a stern look, planted his hands on the carpet, and looked at me. He scraped his face and stood. He told me once that in Brazil there is no racism. The people there were so mixed a good woman could knock out three kids with the same man and get three flavors of coffee in no particular order. I walked over to my friend, spread my arms, and he hauled me off the ground like a bear. He put me down and gave me a look, up and down.

Rhino had been too old to make real money when the UFC had first started to make mixed martial arts a moneymaker. He'd fought professionally in vale tudo fights in Brazil and Japan, back when vale tudo still meant that anything goes. He'd trained fighters to be in the UFC and in the Japanese Pride Fighting events. Time had passed, but Rhino was still on top as a trainer; the real fighters knew him and what he was.

Rhino knew the game, and he knew the game I was working on. I was not a kid looking for a favor; I was here on business, and I wanted to talk. He waved at the man who'd walked me over, and that dude was gone. Rhino opened the door behind him, and I followed. I knew the gig. The door shut, and my focus was on him. He slid into a chair. Gave me a wave. I sat.

"Nickel. Where have you been? Long time."

"I've been working, busy with a few cases."

"You still have much to learn, my friend. You should not be such a stranger to jiu-jitsu."

"I know. I'm sorry."

"Why do you come today?"

"I need to hire somebody."

"Have you used anything we worked on?"

"Yes."

"What?"

I thought about that. There wasn't a day that went by that I didn't use something I'd learned on the mats or in the classroom with Rhino; that was the kind of impact he had on a student. Once you started training, you never stopped thinking the way he wanted you to. He made people into steel out of flesh and bone.

"Caught a guy in a heel hook. He didn't know the rules. Walks with a cane now."

Rhino pushed his chair aside; I stood and did the same. I knew this was how it would play.

"Show me."

I grabbed his shoulder and spun him so he faced away. Put my right leg between his and threw my weight against his shoulder. Rhino spun with me—he was letting me move him, I had no illusions about that—and we landed sitting in front of one another, his leg in my lap. I tucked his foot in my armpit and turned. Rhino tapped a drumbeat on my leg, and I let him go. It was a move he never would have given up to in the cage. If we'd been really fighting, not only would I have not been able to tap him out, we'd still be standing—Rhino was nearly impossible to get to the ground unless he wanted you there.

"He no tap?"

"No."

Rhino stood and brushed himself off.

"You takedown sloppy. Submission is strong. Strong like man." He smiled. "Not like Rhino, though."

I shook my head. I would never be like Rhino.

"This man, he deserve it?"

We sat and I nodded, thought about catching the window peeper outside of an eight-year-old girl's bedroom. Saw the bulge in his pants. Went to him with no fear; I knew he'd be weak. He was. I left him screaming, knee destroyed. The police found him there, didn't believe a word of what he said about a little boy in all black who knew how to make a man feel like a pretzel. They found knives, a tool to cut glass with, some ether. It might not have been the night yet, he could have still been working up to it, but either way, he had it coming. Rhino clapped his hands together and said, "That's good then, very good. Why you see me today?"

"I need someone strong in jiu-jitsu, but this person can't look strong."

He nodded.

"This person will need to be in a fight, maybe a couple of fights. The guy that he fights, he has good hands, walks like a boxer. No kicking, some Thai boxing. I don't think he knows about the ground."

"Does he have honor?"

I knew what Rhino meant. Would Jeff have a weapon? Would he know when a fight was over? I thought about the fight with Dewayne, Jeff watching to see if he was okay. I nodded my head yes, he had honor.

"When?"

"Today. Just a couple of hours."

"Where?"

I told him.

"I have heard they fight there. Children, no training. This boy, he a good fighter?"

"Yes."

"How much?"

"I can pay a thousand on it. If you get this boy to be the kind of fighter I think he can be, I get my thousand back as a finder's fee."

I took the money from my wallet and slid it across the table. He considered it for a moment and made the money disappear. He leaned back in his chair. Rubbed his hands together. He stood. I followed him from the room. We walked back to the gym. He led me to the ring, to a skinny man in a gi who looked just out of high school, working a man Rhino's size. Rhino raised his eyebrows at me.

"Ricardo."

I nodded. Watched him transition with his much larger opponent from a standing position into an arm trap that led to a submission. The kid moved like a snake, a boa constrictor. He was perfect.

Chapter 15

I rode my bike to Knapp, a long haul but that was alright; it would give me time to think. I should have called Arrow but was glad I hadn't. She liked Jeff; she might not like him as much after he lost. I stuck a matchstick in my teeth. On second thought, I really *should* have called Arrow.

I jumped off the bike. The remnants of a party were everywhere, including at least a hundred bucks in empties—the kegs hadn't been enough. Not too much other trash though, and I had a feeling they left the empties on purpose; somebody will always stop to get a dime. I sat next to my bike and waited, hoping Ricardo would show up before Jeff, hoping Jeff would show up at all. A black pickup truck pulled across the field. Dually tires in the back, crew cab. Rhino. Ricardo got out and walked over to where I was sitting. He still had on his gi. He didn't look nervous or excited. He just looked ready. The truck pulled off. I knew Rhino wasn't going far; he'd want to watch.

Ricardo said, "You're Nickel?"

"Yes."

"Rhino says you're good."

"Not as good as you."

"We should roll sometime."

I replaced my matchstick and tossed the old one on the ground. Ricardo would destroy me if we rolled, but it would be good for me. "Next time I come by. You want to know anything about this guy?"

"Rhino told me what to do."

That was good enough for me. We sat and waited, the sun flirting on the outside of the clouds, just peeking, not coming all the way through. We didn't wait long.

The car was red, a little worn around the edges, a highschooler's car. I knew it was Jeff before he got out. He parked next to the sand pit, and we walked over to him. I was in front of Ricardo. He was leaning on the car by the time we got there, staring at Ricardo and seeing right through me—and the ruse.

"Where's the girl?"

I answered him. "There's no girl."

He nodded.

Ricardo stood next to me and said, "I heard you can fight."

"That's right. I've beaten up a few karetekas. You sure you want to do this?"

He knew why we were there. I wasn't surprised. Ricardo let him think his art was karate; it would make things happen even faster. Ricardo said, "I'm sure."

Jeff stripped off a sweatshirt and the T-shirt underneath it. He stepped into the sand pit. "Let's go."

If Ricardo had any reservations about giving him a go in a pit outdoors, he didn't show them. I could see Rhino's truck behind them. He was probably in it with a pair of binoculars, ready to even things if it went bad, possibly on my end and Jeff's, if I'd been wrong about honor. I watched the two square up less than ten feet away. I threw my matchstick on the ground and grabbed another new one. It was hard to keep from shaking.

Jeff came in with his hands up and clenched into tight fists. There was no caution like there'd been with Dewayne; he went right for it. Ricardo was stiff in a karate stance, faking it for his opponent. When Jeff was close enough, Ricardo threw a teep, or push kick, into his solar plexus. It knocked the younger fighter back. He was surprised and came back swinging, big haymakers that would have ruined Ricardo, but Ricardo wasn't there. As Jeff threw blows into the wind, Ricardo grabbed his legs and drove him into the dirt.

He landed with his knees on Jeff's left side, and then he quickly transferred, holding Jeff's left wrist all the while, and tossed his legs over Jeff's prone body. A shark on his feet, Jeff couldn't even swim on the ground. Ricardo bent his arm in the way opposite of its intent, and Jeff screamed and smashed his fist rapidly on Ricardo's hip. Ricardo let him go slowly and stood. Jeff came up next, slowly, unsure of what had just happened. Ricardo said, "Jiu-jitsu."

Jeff nodded. Put his hands up. Ricardo smiled and waved him in. Different submission that time, same result. Ricardo caught him in a wrist lock, or kimura. They stood, and this time they shook hands. Ricardo said, "Let me see your hands—let your hands go into the air."

Ricardo looked to the fields to be sure Rhino could see from the truck. Jeff punched a kata of strikes into the air, tight combinations of head-crushing trauma. He stopped, looked at Ricardo. They smiled. Behind them, I could see the truck moving. We watched it come in, slow but sure. Rhino stopped it near to us and got out, walking a heavy plodding pace that in no way showed how agile he could be. Ricardo walked to stand next to him, and Rhino said, "Now you fight against jiu-jitsu, is different fight for you."

"Yes."

"Who teach you strikes?"

Jeff swallowed thickly. "I do."

Rhino and Ricardo shared a glance. Rhino said, "Show me two more combinations. Punch the wind, boy, let yourself go."

Jeff did it, hard strikes that were thrown from the hips and not the arms. Jab, cross, body. Jab, body, hook. Jab, jab, uppercut, body. Rhino held up his hand.

"You good, boy, you could be real good—could be fighter. Who knows, right? What you need is ground fighting, you need kickboxing. Now you are this."

Rhino held up his fist.

"But you could be like this."

He extended the same hand, palm open now.

"If you can fight anywhere, no problems for you. A man he have kicks, you take him down, twist him. Man better at you on the ground, you stay up, punish him with what God give to you. You work hard, you could be something. You no work hard, you can be nothing… You watch UFC?"

Jeff nodded, his eyes as big as dinner plates.

"True warriors. I train UFC fighter sometimes; Nogueira brothers, they come sometimes, others too. To share and learn, to test each other. You keep up the street fighting, is no good for you. Someday you hurt somebody, go to jail. Or maybe you get hurt?" Rhino shrugged. "Doesn't matter, right? Either hurt or caged like a dog. But you train in a gym, you fight in the ring or the cage, you not get hurt. Not real hurt. You no go to jail; you go in yourself, to see how much good you can pull out. There is only one problem. Street fight. I cannot train fighter who fights out of the ring. Then I get in trouble with you. You train with me, you learn."

Rhino tapped his temple twice and then swung his arm so fast I couldn't even see it, clipping the matchstick from my teeth and lighting it across his shoe.

"You don't train, you gonna burn."

He threw the match on the ground and stomped it out. My hands were trembling next to my pockets, and air was heaving in and out of my chest. Jeff said, "When can I start?"

"You want to start, we start now. Today."

"How much will it cost to train?"

"To start, nothing. We see how you are, how quick you learn. If you do well, we sign contract for you to train to be a fighter. A real fighter. Real fighters teach classes, train with other real fighters, help run my gym. Real fighters fight someday, for my gym. If you're not a real fighter, that's okay, you still train, you work to be a real fighter. You'll pay, but not much."

Jeff was smiling, both his eyes and his mouth.

"I want to do it, no more fighting."

He turned to look at me.

"Who's he?"

Rhino smiled broadly so I could see his teeth. "You'll never know his name, but he do the best thing for you since your mother made you. Now, you get in your car; Ricardo can go with you, show the way."

Jeff picked up his shirts, and Ricardo clapped him across the back. I could see Jeff almost stumble from the blow, and then he wrapped his arm around Ricardo's back as well. They already looked like brothers. I took a match and tossed it in my teeth; I don't think my hands shook.

Rhino said, "You call the boy's mother, send her to the gym. She'll have to sign him up."

"Okay."

"Thank you for letting me meet him, Nickel. You'll see your money back—kid has power, real power. You come back to the gym; you're not bad yourself, but you could be better."

"I will, Rhino, I just have to wrap some stuff up first."

He was already climbing into his truck, waving. I'd never see that money; guys like Rhino don't call you to give back cash. That was okay, Veronica would give me the G plus some change. Walking to the bike, I almost felt like I'd been in a fight. Time to go home, relax for a minute. Call Arrow, have her over. Tell her about me. Tell her about her—maybe even tell her about some imaginary us.

Yeah right, I needed to get groceries and get to work; I have a business to run. Sucks, and I still needed to get closer on Shelby. I was convinced she was dead, but either way she needed finding. The police weren't doing anything, yet on the other hand, neither was I. It was a lot to think about—Four Oaks, Shelby, everything.

Chapter 16

I left the field and went straight to the gas station near Knapp and called Veronica.

"Hello?"

"This is Nickel. Can you talk?"

"Yes! God, I was hoping you'd call! Last night Jeff came home with his eye about knocked out of his head! He had blood all over him and he was drunk, I could smell it. You said you were going to be watching him this weekend, and I have no idea where he is right now!"

I let her get it all out; the phone was off of my ear by almost a foot. When she sputtered the last of it, I said, "Veronica, babe, he's fine. Problem solved."

"Where is he? What happened?"

I told her, let her know how it was done, let her know she was on the hook for seventeen hundred, and let her know where she needed to go to sign her kid up to learn to be a man. She thanked me, said she'd send the money, and I hung up the phone. I didn't need two women in my life anyways.

Chapter 17

I thought about Arrow on my way home to get a backpack, on the way from my house to the store, and while I wrapped up my bike. I shook her out of my head and went in to buy some food. She was hard to shake. The skirt last night hadn't helped, and neither had the top or her taking my arm for a second as we walked to the party. I gave up, let Arrow have a quarter of my head and used the rest to get groceries.

When you're a kid like me, you really need to know how to grocery shop. It's not as easy as you'd think—certainly not as easy as it is for a civilian.

First off, you need a game plan. I have two. Either you need to be shopping for a meal, like a pack of pork chops, stuff for a marinade, stuff for a salad, things like that. The other way is to shop to fill holes, forget that you don't have a mom and imagine she needs to make a cake and needs a couple of things. I usually top a trip like that with a bag of chicken nuggets or a pizza, like maybe the parent in question is busy and just wants a quick meal.

Whichever plan it is that I pick, I always start the same way, in the magazines. I used to shop at a store really close to my house called D&W. When they closed, I had to shop at Meijer full time. The nice thing they had was comic books. Not all good ones—most were *Archie* and *Jughead*, and those suck—but the fact is, they had comics, Meijer doesn't. In any case, the first rule of thumb is to hang out in the magazine aisle touching stuff. You don't leave until you get noticed. A thirty-year-old guy could read *Field and Stream* once a month on his grocer's shelf until he died; a kid couldn't see two pages without getting the eye. Kids spill, make messes—we're held to a higher standard. Always, magazines first, then get to shopping once the glares from employees start.

After that, just do everything as fast as possible—you've got bigger fish to fry, you're a kid! Rush around the store, but don't make them think you could be shoplifting or make them ask you to stop running. You want to attract attention for doing kid things, but you don't want to actually involve the real ire of an adult. It's like being on safari in Africa. You want to see the lions, not get eaten by them. The goal is to buy groceries and get out, not make somebody wonder why that kid is always in here shopping, maybe call a cop to follow you home.

The last thing I always do is spend a lot of time while I wait in line admiring the candy, finally picking out something for myself. For some reason, this lulls adults into dreaming about how wonderful being a kid is, makes them feel there with you. The reason is that they're not a kid like me. I don't want them to be concerned for my well-being; I want them to leave me alone. Nobody worries about a kid whose biggest problem is picking whether he wants almonds or not.

Usually, you end up with either a rude cashier or one who wants to be cool and talk to you like you're an adult. I'm not sure which kind is worse. What I do know is that the sooner you're out of the store the better. Get outside, load your backpack as discreetly as possible, and bust out of there. If I could stand the idea of a basket, that would help, but vanity insists I avoid that route.

I actually bought one of those bike trailers that little kids ride in to haul my stuff but never used it. I thought it would be a little too eye-catching. It's a pain, honestly, the whole mess—I just want to get in and get my crap like anybody else.

Today went off without a hitch. I read a *Star Wars Insider* magazine, seriously, got ocularly screamed at by a manager, and got to work. I bought milk, eggs, a pack of link sausages, and a sack of frozen chicken tenders. Ended up topping my stuff with a Snickers and endured a banal conversation with the cashier about how school was going and if I was excited for snow. It was going just fine, considering I wasn't going, and who in their right minds liked snow? I lied on both counts, left the store, loaded the bike, and went home.

It was late afternoon by the time I rolled into the driveway. I brought my stuff in and loaded it all up into the refrigerator and freezer. Took some chicken tenders out and threw them on a pan, preheated the oven. I plugged my pager into the charger and sat at my computer desk. Flexed my fingers out to crack my knuckles. Went fishing. Popped up like a cork when the oven beeped. Loaded my food in, went back to work. Missed a page, ignored it. Missed another one, the oven beeped, and I had a fish on. Fish left before I could get enough info to make his life change for him. Took my food out of the oven, plated it, added barbecue sauce. Checked the pager. Arrow. I ate and called her on line five.

"Hello?"

"Arrow."

"I thought you were going to call me."

"I had to move fast; I didn't have time."

"Did it work?"

"Yes."

"Can we meet tonight?"

"How soon?"

"Six. You know where."

She was getting good—too good.

"I'll be there."

She hung up. I stuck the pager in my pocket and went in the kitchen to wash the plate and baking sheet. I finished, got on the bike, and left. She was waiting when I got there, and so was Eyepatch. She wore purple jogging pants and a taut Adidas T-shirt under a just-zipped hoodie.

"What's going on?"

"I want to ride through Four Oaks with you again."

"Sounds good; let's go."

We waved at Eyepatch together and unhooked our bikes. She led, and I followed. She was angry, I could see it in her posture. I wasn't surprised—if anything, I'd been waiting for it. I pedaled hard and caught up to her. I said, "Tell me."

She braked and her bike stopped violently, throwing down a black tire track, a bicycle's fingerprint. Now that I was next to her, I could see that Arrow's eyes were wet with tears. The storm had come. Shelby's disappearance had nothing to do with it; I imagine the warning signs had been there for years. The girl leaving was just the last of it, the proverbial straw.

"He left her. I knew he'd leave her. I could hear them yelling at each other. My mom was drunk, and my dad was worse than drunk. He was vicious. He hates her. He hates me."

"Did he hurt Shelby?"

"No. Not like that. He used to paddle us when we were younger, but that was it. He told my mom that she got pregnant just to latch on, just to keep him around. He was talking about her having Shelby just to keep the family together, to hold onto him and his money. You know what she said? She told him it was true and that if she could, she'd do it the same way again. That it was all worth it now that she knew how miserable he'd been. He said she could see him in court.

"I didn't want to listen anymore because I knew what was coming, just like I think Shelby would have known if she'd been there. He was careful, but not careful enough, you know?"

I nodded and let her finish. She was spitting out poison, and if she didn't get it all out it would fester like venom from a snakebite.

"My mom started talking quietly, not so I couldn't hear but so that she knew he'd have to digest every word. She said that she couldn't wait to see him in court, couldn't wait to see his whore there either. Told him she'd known since the beginning and that she had pictures. She started laughing; it was the most horrible sound I've ever heard."

I hope I wasn't the one who'd gotten her those pictures. Adults don't usually hire me for that sort of thing, but I'd still done a good share of it over the last year or so because of that universal truth, people look through kids, they think we don't see. I guess most of the time they're right, but an observant kid who keeps his head down and his mouth shut, a kid like that can learn a lot. You can trust me on that.

"She told him she didn't care about the whore, that he could have a hundred whores if he wanted to, to her it was all the same. She told him if she brought him to court she would take everything. He left, saw me in the hallway. He had to have known I'd heard everything. He said he'd be back. He had a little bag with him, and I think he probably will be back, but I don't even care. I wish I was dead like Shelby."

"You don't know that Shelby's dead."

"Nickel. She's been gone ten days. She's not coming back."

"Either way, we're going to find her. I'm going to find her."

"'Either way'?" I'd only partway agreed with her—I'd just spoken as though it was a possibility that her sister might not be found alive—but she looked at me with a puzzled look on her face, and I wasn't sure if she was going to hug me or hit me. She picked the latter.

It's not good luck to get punched off of your bike into some-body's lawn, but it's a sure sight better than landing in the road. My bike was twisted up in my legs, and I did a mental check of my extremities—everything seemed in proper working order and still attached. Arrow's head moved over me and blotted out the sun.

"Are you okay?"

"I think so."

"I'm sorry I hit you."

Not sorry enough, I guarantee that. Arrow had really gotten off a good one at the expense of my already not-so-pretty face.

"It's alright."

She offered me a hand, and I took it. I let her start pulling me up, but halfway there I froze.

"Quit fooling around. Let me help you up."

"Arrow." My voice was cold. She stopped pulling, and I let go of her hand. "Arrow, are there telephone poles and lines all through Four Oaks?"

"I think so. Why?"

I thought hard, put the boot print by the hair band into my head. Turned it, twisted it. I could see the marks that hadn't been on any of the boot pictures I'd seen on the Web, the deep marks of climbing equipment worn into the earth. Was Shelby a victim of opportunity, or had she been watched, maybe even talked to by her kidnapper? It didn't matter. I knew. I didn't need anyone to tell me I was right or wrong on this, I just knew.

"We need to go to the bridge where she was taken."

I stood. She nodded at me and gave my face a sympathetic look. Crap, black eye. She leaned over and kissed me on the cheek. I'd take a bullet for this girl; all she'd have to do is ask. She said, "Let's go."

We rode side by side. She'd gotten out what she'd needed to, and now we could get back to this thing. What I told her was true: dead or alive, we were going to find Shelby.

Chapter 18

We stopped at the bridge and parked our bikes. Unlike the last time, we didn't hop down the hill. Instead, we looked up. Telephone lines, just like we knew there'd be; we'd followed them here. I climbed down the little hill to the creek and looked up. There was a pole right in my line of sight, and I wasn't five feet from where I'd found the hair band. If someone had been up there, they would have known how secluded this spot was. Everything was coming together in my head. Not the why yet—the only why I knew would point to a sexual predator, and I didn't want to think that way unless there was no other solution. The how, though, I was getting all of that.

Arrow was just staring at me from the road, and I called her down. She came down the hill with a sure-footedness I hadn't seen the last time when she'd offered me a hand. I sure hope when I'm older I understand women better than I do now. When she was next to me we did the creek walk again, hurried this time. What we were looking for wasn't in the woods; it was on the other side of them.

We walked past where the shoe had been found and where both of us were convinced Shelby had been dragged against her will. Little sounds came before sights, just small hints of noise as

86

the modern world conquered the sanctity of the woods. We left the trees together and saw what I knew we'd find: telephone poles and wires going in all directions, as far as the eye could see.

"You think someone who works on those lines did it."

"I'm convinced of it."

"Why? Couldn't someone have just seen her and decided to grab her?"

I shook my head.

"Anyone that impulsive is going to have gotten caught before, probably more than once. This guy is used to people seeing through him. He does his work where people live, and he's not a distraction—he's barely an afterthought. He would have time to get ready, to see what people were doing, find the best spot, time, and candidate. He got all of his ducks in a row while the people that live here went about their lives. He was invisible; he always is when he's in uniform. I bet he never even considered that part of that uniform could lead us to him."

"Can we look on the sex offender database for him?"

"He won't be there. Telephone repair work would be like a government job—if you have a record, you aren't getting hired. I imagine if we could look at youth records we'd find him, but those aren't for our eyes."

"So what are we going to do?"

"I don't know yet. I need to think. It's close, just like seeing the telephone lines. I just need to put the rest of the pieces together."

"Do it soon."

"I need to go home."

"So do I."

She gave me a sad smile—home was the last place she wanted to be. A part of me wished I could have her over to the house and order a pizza. It was impossible, the survivor side of me screamed, no one can know where you live. Trust can get you killed. Survivor always won.

"I'll ride with you home."

We pedaled slowly, dawdling as we made our way back to Arrow's shattered home. I had nothing to say on the subject, and she never challenged me to talk. I could feel the skin around my eye puffing up. I'd ice it when I got home. When we turned onto her street, I saw the cops. My blood was ice.

"Arrow, you have to go the rest of the way on your own."

"Why?"

"The cops are at your house. I can't talk to them; questions will get asked that I can't answer."

"They're here because they found Shelby and she's dead." She said it coldly, no malice, just fact.

"Or maybe they found her alive. Either way, you need to face it. Call me when you know what's going on. We can meet tonight if you need to."

"Thank you, Nickel. For everything."

"I'll talk to you soon."

She barely looked human as she rode to her house. I'm sure it felt like she was dying, the life she knew was dying. That was the only easy part about being me. Everything bad had already happened. Something could happen to mirror it, but nothing worse was going to happen to me again. My job was to make the really bad things not happen to other people, and so far I was failing Arrow. It was enough to make a boy chew on a matchstick, so that's what I did.

Chapter 19

When men hunt ducks, they yell, "Quit!" into a little nozzle, and it sounds like quacking. I needed my own quit—I needed to call in my game. If I was going to find Shelby, I had to call my prey by its name. Yell with a voice it understood, a voice it wanted to choke in person.

I started with three of the more popular pedo bulletin boards. Trying was a stretch; I'd thought about these before, but the idea of her being a passable commodity just never occurred to me. I went fishing with a decent-sized lure, man looking to swap lunch in the Midwest. The stuff I didn't say in writing was that I was in possession of a girl older than ten and younger than fifteen. Lunch. Still better than breakfast, but not by much; pedos have bad appetites. I got nothing—found guys looking to swap, but squat in Michigan. I knew it was a long shot. Nothing named Shelby, or matching her description. Logged off, made dinner. Heard the pager go. Called her on line one.

"Nickel."

"Shhh."

"I need you now."

Just tell me where, baby.

She did. I left, on my bike, into the black.

Chapter 20

We met at Knapp—dark, no fights tonight. She was wearing the same kind of sweat suit I was; this was a long trip on a bike. Arrow cut to business quickly.

"They arrested my dad. He beat up his…girlfriend, and she called the cops. Nickel. They found a magazine under his spare tire, a magazine about girls. Young girls. They found Shelby's other shoe too. They think my dad killed her."

She dove into my chest, sobbing. She bounced off of me, and I handled her as best I was able. She was a kite, and I held on to the string. I thought she was wrong, but it wasn't the time to tell her yet. She looked at me with these huge eyes, and I wondered, not for the first time, why everything can come down so hard on a kid.

"Arrow…"

"What?"

"Do you think your dad did it?"

"No."

"Do you think it would even be possible for your dad to have done it?"

"Anything is possible."

"I don't believe this is possible, and I don't even know your dad. If anything, this is just more proof of what we were already thinking."

"How?"

"Somebody had to plant that stuff, right? Someone who would know the perfect time, who would know that they wouldn't be seen."

"You still think some repair guy did this?"

I nodded. She grabbed me around the waist and held me close, a lone anchor in a bad storm. I needed to find our boy, and soon. I needed to find Shelby, and I had no idea how to find my target. So close but so far. I held Arrow as the night overtook us. Don't worry, I know she was only holding me because I was the only one there. That doesn't mean that I couldn't enjoy the company.

When she let me go, we walked back to our bikes. It was late, and she had school in the morning. I saw two cars pass and wondered if the cops had followed her out here. It wasn't likely, but who knew? I pushed the thought aside and got on my bike.

"Call me tomorrow."

"I will."

"Arrow?"

"Yeah?"

"Don't watch TV."

She nodded and left, disappeared right in front of my eyes. I took the long way home, trying to think. I got a page when I was halfway home, same number that I missed a couple days ago. On a whim I stopped at the post office. One envelope. I tucked it in my back pocket, tucked my chin against my chest, and ducked out of there. No creeps. I went home. I was still thinking about how to find the repairman when I fell asleep. I called the number the next morning.

Chapter 21

A woman answered on the second ring.

"Hello?"

She had a raspy voice, whiskey and cigarettes would be my guess.

"You paged me."

"This is Nickel?"

"We can't talk like that on the phone."

"I need to talk to you."

I thought about Arrow, her father in chains, mother a mess, sister still missing. "I don't have time for anything right now."

"This would be worth your time. I need someone with your skill set."

The survivor in me spoke. "How long will it take?"

"A couple of days, tops."

"When can you meet?"

"Tonight."

"Downtown library. Seven o'clock. Come alone. Wear a baseball cap; go stand by the Stephen King books in fiction."

She hung up on me. The hair on my neck stood on end. I set the phone back on the receiver and went to my computer.

You'd think it'd be hard to find employee records on the phone company Web site, but within ten minutes I found buried in there a handy alphabetical listing of all our fair city's line maintenance personnel. Just names, unfortunately. Names were no good, or at least not enough. I was going to need to take a risk, see who showed up and then use this database to find them. If I got lucky, I'd get our guy. If there were a way to know that the same repairman would be back, I'd head over there right now and cut down a telephone pole. That wouldn't work more than once. People would be wise the next time they heard a saw. I needed creativity. Moved my mouse, clicked a few buttons. Started looking for answers.

A couple of years ago I read an old comic that made a joke about how there was a magazine for everything. With the digital world at our fingertips, the joke is over—there really is content for everything. What I was looking for didn't take long. These days even lumberjacks take time to get out of the woods and onto a laptop.

I found what I was looking for after just a few minutes: stump removal. Not fire, that wouldn't work, but explosives, that was fine with me.

There were no diagrams for exactly what I needed to do, but there were plenty of descriptions on how a similar task had been accomplished. I just needed to figure out angles to maximize impact on a small area. If I was going to take down a telephone pole, I didn't want it falling on someone's house. It came to me; I went to the garage to work.

Dug into my workshop that I've cobbled together over the years and closed the garage. Looked at my pipe lengths and decided on a six-inch piece of galvanized steel, inch and a half in diameter. I made a hole using an eighth-inch drill bit in the length of it. Took red Loctite and screwed on one end cap, also galvanized steel. I plugged in my hot glue gun, let it warm.

When the glue was running, I took my cannon fuse and cut a six-inch section of wick. I slid it into the hole I'd drilled. It fit well. Took the wick out, filled the hole with the glue gun. Pushed the wick in, more glue around the base. I set it to cool and got out some gunpowder.

The first few pipe bombs I made more to amuse myself than for any real gain. I was experimenting, and I'd already realized that knowing how to make an explosion could prove useful, especially if what I wanted to happen with my life really did come through. I was closer now than I had been then, but the same rules applied now. Do this wrong, wind up dead.

I filled the pipe with pistol gunpowder. I use the strongest they make; I always keep a couple of cans in the garage, plus one in the house. You never know when something might need to go bang. I poured the gunpowder in, hands shaking as the little black granules filled the tube. When it was done, I put more red Loctite on the pipe and threaded on the other cap. I brought it inside the house with me, let it sit on the kitchen table. Went out back, watered the plants. I came in and was going to go to the basement but changed my mind. I walked into the kitchen and checked my pager three times. No Arrow.

I fiddled around online when I got back into the office—nothing, nobody was biting. I took a shower and went to the library. Looked at the pipe bomb on the table. Pure evil.

Chapter 22

I saw her immediately, waiting for me just like I'd told her to. She had black hair, thick—made you want to run your hands through it. Pale, milk-white skin. Eyes as black as her hair. Dressed in all black, sweater that came halfway down her arms, leather skirt cut mid-thigh. She looked like she had died but was still warm. She followed me outside without saying a word. When we were off of the steps to the library, she said, "So you're Nickel?"

"Yep."

"I've heard good things."

"I hope not. What things?"

"Nothing specific, just that you're reliable."

"So what do you need help with?"

She took a cigarette out of a pack in her purse. I had a match out to light it before she could react. She pulled long off of it and blew the smoke; I watched it dissipate under the glow of the streetlight. I tossed the match into the gutter. She took something else out of her purse and handed it over. I held it to the light. A hundred-dollar bill.

"Fake?"

"Yes."

"It's a good fake."

"Yes."

"So what do you want me to do with it?"

"I need to get it cleaned."

"How much?"

"A hundred and fifty thousand to start. If I can get thirty-five cents on the dollar, I'd be a happy girl."

"Twenty-five."

"Thirty."

"End up at about forty-five thou?"

"That's right. Thing is though, if we can build a good enough network, this can happen all the time."

"Can you get anything smaller?"

"Why?"

"Smaller is easier. If you had that money in tens, maybe even twenties, it'd be a cinch."

"These are already printed."

"Won't do you much good if you get caught."

"You'll be doing the work. Everything I've heard about you seemed to indicate that you don't get caught."

The lady made a good point.

"Alright, I'll work on it. I don't want any weight until I can figure out what I'm going to do with it."

"Fair enough. How long?"

"Give me a week; things are crazy right now."

"Do you get a hold of me, or…"

"Is the number you paged me at good?"

"Yes."

"Then I'll call you once I get this thing figured out."

"I hope that you're going to take this as seriously as it needs to be taken."

"That's the only way I take anything. I understand the apprehension, but this is just another job for me, miss, and when it's done, there'll be another job after it."

She extended her hand, and we shook. She took her arm back, flashed me a grin, and spun to leave. Still had plenty of shake from what I could tell as she walked away. I checked the pager. No Arrow. I went home; I had work to do. It was going to be a long night.

Chapter 23

I was happy to see the pipe bomb still sitting on the table. I suppose the lack of police cruisers around the house should have tipped me off first. I checked the clock, went back outside to the garage. Started putting my kit together.

Cordless drill, full charge, Sawzall, full battery there, too. A length of rope, maybe twenty feet. Gorilla glue. Air horn. One-inch drill bit. A pair of night vision goggles with a 1×3 magnification reticule set in the lenses. A little LED flashlight. A rubber mallet and a wooden dowel sawn off to work as a punch. Matches already in my pocket. A wish that Arrow would call. Went back in the house, lay down on the couch. Thought better of it and went to bed. Set the alarm for two.

I woke confused, the alarm screaming at me. I remembered Arrow and Shelby and shut off the alarm. Went to the bathroom, painted my face with makeup, shades of black, gray, and brown. I looked at myself. I was a demon. Got dressed in all black, non-reflective clothing. Grabbed the bag with all of my stuff and threw it over my shoulders. Got the pipe bomb last and strapped it to my thigh with tape. If it went off, I wanted it to kill me, not leave me a cripple. I took a deep breath and rode my bike to Four Oaks; the only light was the moon. I rode past the gas station. It was closed, so no worries about being seen. I rolled into Arrow's neighborhood and tucked the bike behind the first truly dark tree that I saw. When I left it, I made sure to stay close to houses so I could bolt if I needed to. Nice night, if you weren't a runaway with ten ounces of gunpowder strapped to your leg.

What I needed, besides a telephone pole, was a nearby sewer grate and a good spot to sit and hide. I needed to watch, see who showed up besides police and fire trucks. I had a vibe that tonight I might get to see the man who took Shelby. I checked my pager, more out of habit than anything else. Still nothing from Arrow. I veered off of my path, stopped looking for what I needed, and went to her house. Her light was on, but I still felt silly throwing pebbles at her window, like I was some hapless kid in an eighties sitcom. After a couple of stones, her window opened. She popped out.

"Nickel?"

"Who else?"

"I can't see you."

I flicked the flashlight on and off twice.

"You're all black."

"I'm working."

"Shelby?"

"Yeah. Want to come?"

"What are you doing?"

"Nothing I need help with."

Just blowing up your neighborhood.

"No thanks then—I need to study and get some sleep. I was at the jail trying to see Dad pretty much all day. I got like fifteen minutes after he was done talking to Mom and his lawyer. He's a wreck, but I believe that he didn't hurt Shelby."

"Good, he didn't. There's going to be a big bang within the next half hour or so, okay? Don't mess yourself."

"Thanks for the heads-up."

"We're going to have work to do soon. Call me."

"I will."

She slid the window shut, and I slunk off into the black, feeling more like a ninja than a little boy playing private eye. I found the perfect pole just after I left Arrow's, right by a sewer grate on a plain stretch of road. It was far enough away from the house in front of it that even if it blew bad it probably wouldn't hit it. Most importantly, there were no lights on around me, either on the streets or on either of the closest two porches. I took a deep breath and knelt next to the pole, sliding my backpack off of my shoulders and laying it in the lawn.

I took the night vision goggles out first and snapped them onto my head. I closed my eyes and switched them on. My pupils dilated under my eyelids, and I opened my eyes to see. The world was built in shades of yellow and greenish light. I took the drill, pulled the trigger, and let it hum for a second. I picked my spot on the pole and went to work.

It was harder work drilling into the telephone pole than I'd expected. I had a terrible time getting even halfway in, and I was worried about wearing out the bit or bending it. I made six holes in the pole, one on top of another so the edges were touching. I put the drill in the backpack and got the saw. Throwing what I knew about carpentry aside, I pushed the saw into the hole before turning it on. It whined a little, but the blade didn't snap as I cut the treated lumber, widening the channel for my bomb. Satisfied with my work, I put the saw down next to the bag and tore the bomb off of my leg. I was close but not there yet. I set the bomb in the bag and made two more cuts. I tried again, and it fit, just barely.

I put the saw away and got out the hammer and bit of dowel. Slowly hammered at the dowel to push the bomb the rest of the way in the hole. It cinched it in perfectly; I wouldn't need the glue after all. I shoved the hammer and dowel into the bag and grabbed the rope. I wrapped one end around the pole about five or six times, just above the bomb, and tied it off. The other end I tied to the sewer grate, pulling on the rope to make what little tension I could force on the pole. Once the rope was as taut as I could get it, I stepped back to admire my handiwork. Everything looked in order, so I threw the backpack on and switched off the night vision. I sat next to the pole to let my eyesight reacclimate to the black night and lit a match on my belt buckle. I stuck it to the fuse and backed away. If I'd done the math right, the bomb would go in about seven minutes. If I'd done a really nice job, the pole would fall when it exploded. I backed into the safety of the bushes of the closest house, the goggles atop my head and the flashlight in a shaking hand.

Sitting alone in the night, waiting for an explosion that was going to take forever to come, I hoped for Shelby's sake that I was right. Arrow and Shelby, lives in limbo—and if I was wrong, no end to that limbo in sight. This was a long shot, but as best I could calculate, it was our best chance. I could see the fuse humming and bouncing under the light from the moon and the suburbs. I waited, and I hoped I was right.

Chapter 24

The explosion was deafening. One second it was a quiet weeknight in the suburbs, the next it was a war zone. The pole leapt off of itself like a horse vaulting a jump. It hung in the air, frozen as the energy from the explosion warred through it. I saw the rope go rigid, expected it to snap, and then the pole fell to the ground. The sounds were barking dogs and security systems, modern watch-dogs for cars and houses. I wondered with a guilty smile how many windows I'd broken. I backed as far away as I could, to the edge of the woods Shelby had disappeared in. I lowered the night vision and flicked it on. I waited.

It didn't take long.

Chapter 25

At first, just adults' loud swearing. Related, I'm quite sure, to the destruction of quite a bit of insured glass. Seriously, if there was a person I felt bad for, it was their broker. How someone can get so angry over something broken that will be replaced for free is beyond understanding. Not to mention, I wasn't exactly in the ghetto—these folks had money. I'm sure it was inconvenient that my little project woke somebody up, but seriously, calm down; it's just a pipe bomb.

Little groups of them gathered in yards, separate armies split by the downed and sparking lines. I hadn't even considered the idea that they might be power lines. Phones just seemed obvious—they call them telephone poles. Why hang electrical stuff off of them? In any case, the police were next, great gobs of them to defend suburbia from the mad bomber. If they'd just worked this hard in the first place, maybe Shelby wouldn't still be missing with the wrong man in custody. But what do I know, I'm just a kid.

Fire trucks and ambulances and finally, someone from the electric company. He was heavyset, and he waded through the police barricade—I could tell as he nodded at a couple of the uniforms that this wasn't his first rodeo. I clicked my night vision to the 3× to zoom in on him. It was hard to see his face, but I locked in what I could see. If there were a picture to look at, I'd know it was him. Granted, I had my doubts that the first guy on the scene would be my quarry.

Two more electric company trucks pulled up next, and they had three more faces to recognize. I still thought it was most likely that the person responsible would be a lower-level worker, maybe come out in the days following to repair my mess. Still, having a database of four of them to work from was a good start. Even I can admit, though, the guys doing routine electrical work aren't typically the kind pulled up for disaster time. I kept looking for a phone truck, but none were coming. It was kind of embarrassing, to be honest. I felt my pager buzz, but I ignored it; there was too much going on to worry about missing a call. One more truck pulled in right afterwards. Phone company. Great. Now I had two pools to wade through.

My pager buzzed again. I ignored the stupid thing; somebody needed to get some patience. The cops milled around, laughing and joking. I just watched. I was getting bored, but who knew, something could turn up. The guys from the phone company truck got out, but I only got a look at one. I was trying my darnedest to scope the other guy so I could put another proof in the piggybank when the pager buzzed again. I clipped it off my belt and held it up so I could see it. The lit numbers burned like fire.

911-59 911-59 911-59. The second was the same, and so was the third. The last was Arrow's number with 911. Crap. 5-9. K-9. I saw the car with the dog markings on its side pull in as I ducked into the woods.

Chapter 26

I ran. I ran as hard as I could and as fast as I was able. I had no idea where I was going, and I didn't care. I couldn't go back, couldn't go to foster care or reform school or juvie or any of it. That was not an option; I'd kill myself the first chance I got. I'd promised.

A promise to Nick and Eleanor. A promise to Annette, a promise to the fields behind the house, pregnant with bodies. Where my own corpse was supposed to lie. Where Nick and Eleanor ended up was a mystery to me. They wanted to stay together; I wanted to get gone. I took the money and ran, all of that nasty, dirty sex tape money. I made a life for myself, and it was as hard as I knew it would be, but no cop was going to take it from me. Not today and not ever.

My earliest memory, you don't want to hear about, trust me. It was pain, that should be enough. Pain and shame and a whole lot of other things. My first good memory?

You'd have never known Dad was grieving the way it was with us. It was years later, just before he died, that I learned about his other family, his gone family. I was dropped off as a foster kid, a rent-to-own child. I got the grand tour, and he sat me down at the kitchen table. He was dark black, broad chest with a belly, shaved head with a pencil-thin moustache. Hands as big across the palm as a small pizza. He extended a mitt to shake my hand, and I gave him mine. His huge paw enveloped it, gave me a shake, and let go. He said, "So what do you like to be called?"

I told him.

He nodded and said, "My name is Benjamin. You can call me Ben, or even Dad if it gets to feel right. If you don't mind it here, you can stay for as long as you want. If you don't, you can leave whenever you want to. This house is as open for me as it is for you, with one big difference. I will never kick you out of here. You can leave if you want, but as long as you want to stay, no matter what, you'll be welcome. Do you have any questions you want to ask me?"

I shook my head—I didn't. He was Dad to me less than a month later, a real father. You know the old expression, "You can pick your friends, not your family"? Nothing less true has ever been said. I would do anything to have that moment back again, that wonderful beginning. A good reason why I am what I am. The only good things that happened to me before I was Nickel, the only really good things that ever will. There are so many things I would ask. But there are even more I would tell him.

Dad showing me how to rack the .22 long rifle by myself. My little fingers kept slipping off of the action, and I was getting frustrated. He wasn't. Just kept saying, "Grab it tight, son. Grab it tight and fire it back." I was four at most, but my real age is a mystery to me, and we decided early on that we'd just share the same birthday. I try to tell myself I don't care about stuff before that, and sometimes I even believe it. I was with the woman who birthed me, not my mother, for the first couple years of my life. There are no memories there that aren't miserable. I was with Dad for less than four years; I wish I knew exactly how long. I wish I knew the count by the day.

Sitting in his office, his name on the door. Meeting a girl with a problem, knowing even when I was young that the good parts were getting left out for the sake of my ears. Him standing up for me to a teacher I knew was doing bad things with some of the girl students. She was, but no "biological" parents believed their kids. She was fired; to the best of my knowledge, no one ever thanked my dad. Also to the best of my knowledge, he never cared.

I learned about the family business a little from him, but I mostly used the rules he made for himself as I got older. He never laid them out to me or said in some old-guy talk how a man was supposed to act. I learned the good way. I watched him, listened to how he treated people, to how he let people treat him. "Always open a door for a lady, and always hold one for a fella if he's close." He never said it—I just watched. You could learn a lot from a man who knew how to say please and thank you, yes sir and yes ma'am. People worry about leopards and elephants and tigers being endangered, but we all watch as rudeness butts its way into normal conversation. We should care about the animals, don't take me the wrong way. It's just that we should care about ourselves too.

Dad worked for free a lot, at least as far as I could tell, but we were always getting little things. Not boxes of apples or fried chicken or stuff like in the old days of his work, but sometimes the electric bill would just come up paid, or we'd have cable for a few weeks. Little things Dad didn't care a lick for, but I enjoyed.

He carried a .357 in his jacket. Eight rounds, full-size Smith and Wesson. I wish I had it. Cops took it. You read enough in Detroit, you'll find out that was the gun my dad killed himself with, right after he gave himself two black eyes, broke his own nose, and shot out his right knee. Someday, I'm going back there.

The wind was cold and the trees were knives, blazing my face and showering me with mist from the dew. I ran. In the distance, barking and beams of light so powerful they could blind a man into submission were cutting through the foliage like lasers. I'm not a man, but I'm working on it.

Chapter 27

Some deep instinct in me was screaming to hide, while a force just as powerful begged me not to, to keep running, to never stop, ignoring the cramps as I scoured the ravages at the ends of the earth. I wasn't sure if it would be safer to keep the night vision on or take it off. So far it was the only thing keeping me ahead and away from them, but if one of those million-candlepower bulbs got me in the eyepiece right, I'd drop as hard as if they were firing guns instead of light. I kept moving, deeper in the woods but close enough to see bits of houses. My feet splashed in something; I worried for the noise and then crossed back and over the little tributary twice.

I moved back to the houses, closer to the yards now but still in the tree line. The dogs and lights were no closer or further away than they'd been; they were after me, and that was all that mattered. When I saw what I thought was Arrow's house, I split from the trees. Crossing the yard was going to be the hardest part, and I ran low, moving as fast as I was able while still remaining close to the ground.

When I came out of the woods, I was two doors down from Arrow's house, little houses and ticky-tacky and all that—stupid things really do look the same. I stayed tight to the trees, still close to the ground, still terrified. It had been stupid to stick around.

It made sense at the time, but now it just seemed like the stupid decision of a little kid. I made it through the no-man's-land of her neighbor's lawn and flew into Arrow's yard. We must have some kind of connection, because she was waiting for me at the back door. Hair pinned up with two pencils, wearing a white T-shirt and blue shorts. She looked like an angel, and that was exactly what I needed. She held her finger over her lips, making the universal sign for, "If you're loud, I'm going to kill you." I abided and followed her in.

The house was dark, and even through the blinds we could see flashlights cutting the night. I shut off the night vision and flipped them up onto my head. Arrow looked at me like I was crazy and whispered, "What are you, freaking James Bond?"

"I need to see at night sometimes."

"You need those."

"They're pretty cool."

"Boys and toys."

"Do you want to try them on?"

"Yes."

I handed them to her, helped her fit them onto her head, and flipped them on.

"Whoa. These are awesome."

"Shouldn't you be hiding me somewhere?"

"Hang on. This is seriously crazy. You can see everything."

The lights were getting deeper into the forest, moving away from us. If I'd left a trail, they were off of it. I sat heavily into a well-padded chair and let Arrow play with my goggles. When she had finished amusing herself, she sat on the arm of my chair with the goggles flipped up on her head.

"Is your mom going to come down here?"

"No, Mom is pretty well incapacitated."

I nodded.

"We're going to need to make you a bed."

"Are you crazy? I can't stay here."

"Where are you going to go, Nickel? All they're doing out there is looking for people who shouldn't be outside. Speaking of that, you knocked out my power, didn't you?"

"I thought they were just phone lines. How was I supposed to know they were phone and power?"

She shrugged. "I'm sure there would have been some way of checking."

I blushed, but she couldn't have seen it in the darkness. "Yeah, well, I would have knocked it down either way."

"How'd you do it?"

I told her, and she nodded and listened like it was the most important thing in the world. When I finished, I could see a question still on her lips.

"How is taking away the power going to...you're going to watch them, see who comes around."

"Clever."

"Did you need to knock down a pole?"

"It was the right thing to do. If I would have cut it, they would have just thought it was somebody being stupid. A bomb in a rich neighborhood? All it'll take is one cowboy cop to say terrorist, and this thing is going to be handled."

She nodded like it made sense to her. If she wanted to go along with me, I wasn't going to argue. She slipped the night vision goggles off and handed them to me. I pushed them into my backpack.

"I get to borrow those someday."

"They can zoom in, like binoculars, just not as far."

She rolled her eyes at me—boys and their toys all over again.

"You can sleep down here. Let me get you a blanket."

"What if your mom comes down?"

"She won't."

"But if she…"

Arrow cocked her head to the right, the loose hair left unsecured by the pencils whipping across her face and shoulders. "Are you going to trust me?"

"Yes. Sorry."

I watched her leave and come back with her hands full with a down comforter.

"I'd show you how to work the TV, but we don't have power. I have school in the morning; at this rate I can get about three hours of sleep if I really work at it. I'll wake you up before I go."

"Thanks, Arrow, you saved my butt."

"Nickel. You were out there doing what you do for Shelby and me. Thank you."

She gave me that big, beautiful smile that I'd impale myself over and threw the comforter on my lap. I drew it over myself and lay back, knowing that I would never be able to sleep. I was wrong.

Chapter 28

I opened my eyes to an unfamiliar blackness. A flashlight beam crossed over my face, and I flew off of the chair, diving towards the form. I was caught in the comforter, drawing back my arm to attack whoever had brought me to the darkness.

The form spoke: "Nickel. Nickel!"

It flooded back. Arrow. Crap. I picked myself off of her as best I was able and sat Indian-style on the floor. I pulled at the comforter, and an Arrow-shaped form emerged. Her head came out first.

"You better not have messed up my hair."

"Uh…"

She smacked me on the arm, playful, not like the shot that gave me the shiner I still had under my eye.

"It's alright, I can fix it."

"The power is still out."

"Nickel, you exploded a power pole—of course it's still out." Yeah.

"I need to get home," I said.

"I need to get to school."

"You want me to walk you?"

"I get a ride with a friend."

She blushed. A boy. My heart. Destroyed.

"I'll call you after school."

"Don't, I'll call you. I've got a busy day."

"You will call, won't you?"

"Yes. Why?"

"I want to help you spy."

It's amazing how a smile and a kind word can fix even a ruined heart.

"Alright. Call."

She smiled, so I stood and followed her outside. "I'll see you tonight. Oh. Nickel, your face!"

She pointed at the hose. It was cold but better than the alternative. I rubbed my face on my shirt and gave Arrow a look. She responded with a thumbs-down, and I gave myself another shot with the hose, another rub with the shirt. Thumbs-up.

I waved and walked off, cutting between yards to get to the road. I saw two cars before I got to the main drag but didn't look at either. I didn't need to see Arrow with her friend to know it would sting.

I was exhausted by the time I got to my bike. It was unmolested, so I climbed on and got out of there. I didn't realize just how sore I was until I got going, little nagging scratches all over me. I needed a hot shower and some serious time in a bed. I'd get at least one of them, and not the one I wanted the most. I went home.

Went in the house and just threw the backpack on the floor; I'd deal with it later. I stripped down and went to the bathroom. My stomach was rumbling, but it could wait until I'd cleaned up a bit. I turned on the shower and climbed in. It was almost scalding, but felt fantastic. I stayed until the hot water ran out and made some food, fried egg sandwiches. I brushed my teeth and went out back, watered my garden. I needed to trim it again soon. Went downstairs and came right back up; it would have to wait. I found two envelopes in my jeans that I hadn't even opened and thought about my three drop boxes that needed to get checked. I pushed it all aside—the scams, the desire to sleep, everything but Shelby and Arrow.

I dressed in urban camo, jeans and a Clipse T-shirt. Thought about a hat and thought better of it. Went to my backpack, unloaded the contents on the table. Took it out to the garage and loaded it. Binoculars, spotting scope, moleskin notebook, and pre-sharpened pencils, three of them. Grabbed a little burner cell phone that I bought in bulk at a 7-Eleven. Camera tripod for shooting in the prone position, a ghillie suit that I'd modified to fit me like a glove, and a matching hat and face mask for the suit. I looked back in my war closet, grabbed my spare and yet-to-be-modified ghillie suit, and stuck it in as well, with another face mask and hat combo. I went back inside and got my camera.

I've got a Canon frame that I really like; I just needed the right lens. I did a few calculations in my head and figured a 100–400 zoom would be good enough. I grabbed that and the body, hesitated, and squashed the thought—if that wasn't a long enough look, then it really wouldn't matter.

All of my camera parts are painted with a solution called Dura-Coat. Most people use it for guns; I go shooting with it too, just not bullets. I can do a mean headshot though, and sometimes they even fall down afterwards. Of course, that only happens after the spouse gets the pictures. The lens and body I grabbed for this job were printed with a forest-colored digital camo. I stuck a couple of flash cards in my pocket and let the camera stuff be.

I paged Gary right before I left with a code we'd come up with to expect a call at seven o'clock tonight. I wanted to bounce some laundering ideas off of him. Just because I was his guy for pot didn't mean he wouldn't know a good way to get rid of some money. Gary was loyal, but that didn't mean he was devoid of other connections. I checked my watch, slung the bag over my shoulder, and got on my bike, and then I went back to Four Oaks to take some pictures.

Chapter 29

I rode my bike to Arrow's house and parked it next to a power pole. As far as I could tell, the power was still out. Whoops. I walked quickly through her side yard and into the woods. If I could make it to her house in the woods while men and dogs chased me, I could make it in daylight back to the site of the bombing.

I heard the sounds of work long before I was able to see it, and I took the cue as a good indicator to change my camouflage from hapless tween to shrubs. I took off my jeans, sure that Arrow would come walking from behind one of the trees while I was half naked, and pulled on the raggedy custom camo. I slipped the hat and face piece on after I'd zipped the suit. The outfit made me feel like something less than human. This was the first time I'd used it for anything aside from practice, and I felt like I was a big bug wearing it. When the light was plucking in at waist height through the trees, I dropped to my knees and elbows to crawl the rest of the way. I stopped ten feet from the edge of the woods, found a lane to shoot through, checked for insects and ants, and committed myself to the earth.

There were four men from the electric company, two from the phone company, and two very bored-looking uniformed cops. If there were canines or any other specialty units, I'd yet to see them;

I didn't expect I would until it was far too late. I slid my backpack to my position and removed the camera and lens. Keeping my focus on what was in front of me rather than what was in my hands, I assembled the camera and lens. Next, I removed the tripod and put the mess together under my stomach. I took a deep breath and pulled the camera from beneath me. I sighted, gave the lens a try, and looked. I saw everything; 400 was too much gun, by a good minute actually. I rolled back to 350. To three. Perfect. He turned before I could shoot. Dark hair, thin on top, dyed. Home job. The bits he missed were gray. He had an average build, saw some sun. He turned back. I fired. Head shot. One down.

They'd already gotten the old pole out of the ground and were working on getting the new one in when I got there. The wires lay coiled up like black snakes on the lawn, and the whole area was cordoned off with yellow police tape and signs saying things like, "Danger! High Voltage!" They'd actually needed to close the street to do the work. I could see a group of five older men across the road watching the work and undoubtedly talking about how they would have done it differently. I aimed over all of them, letting the camera find their faces. I went back to the workers.

I sighted in on a fat one with guts spilling over his belt, a yellow hard hat, and sunglasses. I watched him for a long time, just his face in the frame. He took off the hat, took off the glasses. Wiped his face. When the arm came down, I fired. Caught him cold, air puffing out of his red cheeks. Two down.

I checked my watch; I'd already been down for a bit. If there was numbness in me, I couldn't feel it. One of them climbed the new pole, spike boots on his feet. He was ruddy like the last one, but not fat. Didn't work outdoors much, I could tell just by looking at him. Didn't matter. Boom.

I shot two more, and they broke for lunch. I crawled back the way I came. Soaked into the forest more than I already was, became a ghost. Packed the camera up still built. Slunk back to Arrow's house. When I got there, I lay my pack next to me and stayed ten feet in the tree line. I closed my eyes and concentrated my internal clock on two hours. I closed my eyes and went away. When I woke, it was three in the afternoon.

I called Arrow.

"Hello?"

"Come out back."

"Nickel?"

"No names."

"I know! It didn't sound like you."

I let myself breathe, took two good strong inhales, and said, "Better?"

"Yes. Be right out."

"I'm in the woods."

I hung up, and a few minutes later she stepped tentatively onto the patio, still dressed for school. She held her hand over her eyes to shield them from the sun and scanned the tree line. I called to her.

"Arrow!"

She snapped on my position and drifted away from it, not believing her ears. She stepped off of the patio and walked to the woods. She slid through the grass and walked into the trees. She was almost standing on me, admiring my backpack, when I grabbed her ankle. She jumped and yelled.

"Nickel!"

I rolled over and looked at her. "Hey."

"You were freaking invisible!"

"No. I just took away my lines."

"Your lines?"

"The way that we identify something as human. Arms, legs, noses. It's why zebras have stripes, why most prey animals have markings on their bodies. It keeps them safe."

"It's cool."

I knelt and started picking through the backpack, pulled out my spare suit and hat, and handed them to Arrow.

"For me?"

"I thought you wanted to come?"

"I do. Hang on." She unfastened the top button of her skirt and said, "Nickel, turn your butt around. If I catch you looking, you're dead."

I turned; got to do what the lady says.

A few minutes later she said, "How do I look?"

"It fits you really well." It did. Everything seemed to fit well on Arrow.

"Does this go over my face?"

"Take your ponytail holder off, then slide down your hair and tuck it into the neck of your shirt."

She did it, slowly, making sure she got it right. I nodded approval, and she flashed me a smile. I pulled the mask part over my face and watched her do the same. I took the camera from the backpack and handed her the bag. I led and she followed.

When we got close, I dropped to a knee and walked low. When we got closer, I crawled. I didn't look to see what she was doing; I just had to assume she was impersonating me as best she was able. I knew she wouldn't be able to imitate my herky-jerky movements that were meant to look as nonhuman as possible, but as long as she was staying prone she'd be fine. I could hear her behind me, but she wasn't loud; she was learning. I got us as close to the tree line as I felt comfortable with and waved her forward.

She was smart and left the backpack behind her. I set the camera down, crawled back, and got the spotting scope and binoculars.

I set up the scope in front of her, working slowly. When it was done, I looked through it and brought the tube to bear on them. Zeroed in, motioned for her to look down it. She did and popped back; I could see the grin through her mask. She gave me a thumbs-up. I readied the camera, and we got to work.

By the time we were done, I'd taken three new heads, all of them ladder boys with spike shoes, all from the electric company. None of them had that desk look—they were tanned, had strong builds. I didn't trust a single one of them. To me, they looked like death. It was dusk before we were back at Arrow's. We changed in the woods, and she went back to her world, I went back to mine. Everything was clicking, and I had work to do.

Chapter 30

I called Gary from the pay phone by Arrow's house. When he answered, I said, "Can you talk?"

"Yes."

"You get that money?"

"Yes. Thank you."

"How's heat?"

"Not bad. They searched my car, came to my house, looked there. Nothing. The principal's the one with heat now. He's got my mom yelling up one side of him and the police chief yelling up the other, because my mom hollered at the chief, too. She's angry, but she's proud that her good little Gary didn't do any of the things those liars said, and she has no problem reminding me of just how proud she is. We had to pray about it four times yesterday. I need to get out of this house!"

"Stay cold, you'll be out and about soon enough. I've got a business proposal for you."

"Alright, what do you got?"

"Say I wanted to move some phony money, 'bout a hundred and fifty K."

"That's a lot."

"It is."

"Is it good?"

"Really good, almost fooled me."

"What do they want on the back end?"

"Forty percent."

"Does that leave anything for us? I've never even thought about this stuff before."

"I'll cut you in for five if you help me get rid of it."

"I can look around. See what's out there. I can't remember anybody ever doing anything like that at school, though."

"Exactly. You got kids that burn money, and the best part is, no one will know where it's coming from."

"Have you thought about selling legit money as funny and making the switch?"

"Too much face time. I want this anonymous and gone."

"It's never anonymous for me. This whole school knows I'm lightning, and nobody's talking, except for about how bad they need a bag. No promises on the money."

"All I'm asking is to think about it. You move it, you'll be looking at about seventy-five hundred."

"If I don't get caught."

"Gary, when have you ever gotten caught?"

"I know, man, it's this heat—it's got me flustered. I'm not used to being in trouble. I'll get over it, and I'll let you know about the money."

"Be in touch."

I hung up the phone before he could respond. If Gary didn't get his spine back, I was going to need to send him a message, remind him that anyone with ten cents of brains can sell grass for me. It wouldn't take much dope flowing to get a school that wanted to get high buying. I could flood it in ten minutes with another Gary. The money was a separate issue; I'd just hoped Gary would have given me something to go on. I left the phone and the gas station, went home to work.

Chapter 31

When I got home I threw the backpack on the table with the rest of my mess, and then I turned on the oven so I could make some more chicken strips. I didn't even care what I ate—I just needed to have something in my belly. I took the camera out and ejected the flash card. I went to the office and plugged the card into the reader and my pager into the charger. Bounced back to the kitchen, turned on the timer, and put the last of the chicken in the oven. I went back to the office and fired up the Web. No scams tonight, I was looking for someone specific. I opened the photo viewer, skipped past the first pictures I'd taken, and went to the ones I'd gotten with Arrow.

The first man I'd gotten two shots of, and the second one had something I'd been unable to see through the camera, a nametag. Right under the words "Consolidated Energy," it said "Clyde." I was practically drooling as I skipped past it without looking at him. I went to the other ones, names on both. Freddy and Hank.

I shrunk the photo viewer and went online, went to the electric company Web site, and after about fifteen screens realized that my foray into the Consolidated Energy database was a dud. I shuffled back to the phone company site, fiddled for a minute, and came up with nothing connective between the two. Crap.

I thought for a minute, stuck a pen in my mouth to disguise my voice, and plugged in line five, and then I dialed the number on their homepage.

I went through about five different option menus and hit 0 on all of them; finally I got an operator.

"How can I direct your call?"

"I need to know who's been on my lawn. This is an outrage."

"What is the nature of your complaint?"

"Some idiot blew up our power over here, and I want to know who's been on my lawn."

"Can I have the account number?"

"I'm at work; I don't have the stupid bill right here."

"Address on the account?"

"1138 Oakway, in Grand Rapids. They're destroying my lawn!"

"Just a moment."

Muzak. So far so good. A few minutes later, she was right back at me.

"Sorry about that, how can I help you?"

"I want to know the name of every one of these idiots so I can report them, and then I want to talk to a supervisor or somebody over there who can tell me why there's all this digging when we have elevated lines."

"I'm not authorized to give out employee information."

"I'm not looking to send a Christmas card; I want a list of who's been on my property."

"Sir, I can't give you any names of exactly who's been in your yard. If you'd like, I can e-mail you a list of the repair personnel that service your area, and then you and someone at the local office can figure out which of them were there."

Fantastic.

"I guess that will work."

I rattled off my e-mail address, let her give me the local number, and hung up. Opening up my e-mail got me nothing; five minutes later, I had mail.

There was only one Clyde. I looked him up on the online phonebook. Boom. Clyde Cunningham, 3415 Fern Boulevard. He was easy; I copied and pasted the info into a Word doc and went looking for the other two. There were two Freds, but only one listed as Freddy. I copied his stuff out of the phonebook too, Freddy Jefferson, 77 Duiker Road. Hank was easy as well, but I took that one the way I had the Freds. There were two Henrys, one listed as Henry "Hank" Phillips, 92 Duiker Road. My hand was shaking as I clicked the mouse to copy. Same street as Freddy; no way it was a coincidence. The oven beeped, and I jumped so hard I knocked over my computer chair. I ignored it, went back to the pictures to see them. They stared back, eyes cold. The pictures did nothing to help me relax. I needed to move tonight. I left the office to eat and think.

The way I figured it, musing over a meal of the finest processed, frozen, and reheated chicken money could buy, was that if they were in it, they were in it together. I didn't know what the twist was, but I figured one, if not both of them, was unmarried. If it was only one, the unmarried guy would have the house with the action. I needed to go to Duiker Road and look around. I let the adrenaline from the find chase any fear or weariness out of me, and I went to the bathroom to take a shower.

Duiker Road wasn't far from my house, ten minutes tops, but it wasn't in exactly the best neighborhood. I prepared my camo accordingly, ripped jeans, Detroit Tigers ball cap, Metallica shirt from a recent tour. Chuck Taylors went on the feet. I pulled the bike out of the garage and rolled out to do some recon. It was warmer than the day before had been, and the sun was shining from what felt like directly over top of me. In my pockets I'd stuck the pepper spray pen, the burner from earlier, and a little point-and-shoot digital camera. I wasn't ready for war, but I didn't expect to be in one. This was just to look. I went back in the house and got the starting pistol and tucked it in my waistband where the sweatshirt would cover it. Now I was ready.

Chapter 32

There were no train tracks to cross, and it certainly wasn't on the other side of town, but something changed as I made my way to Duiker Road. Money, that was the only difference. I noticed it first in the yards: landscaping went out the window quickly, then every now and again you'd see one done up beautifully, fighting the darkness that was going to worm its way in no matter what they did.

Every now and again in this stretch you'd see a house that had given up entirely. Yard littered with children's toys and beer cans, grass unmowed. Cars in the driveway that run on prayers instead of gasoline. The American Dream in the darkest light possible. Here too you'd see candles awash in the sea of black, trying their hardest to keep a normal life in their yard and on their street. I could almost see that light winking out, just as sure as the sun had over my own head not too long ago.

I went through it all, the near slum that suburbia can turn into as swift as a bar argument can go ugly. I wasn't immune; I was used to it. I turned onto Duiker Road and did a quick circuit, rolling past 77 and 92 before coming back. I fastened my bike to a stop sign and walked the road. I could feel eyes on me, but that was normal for suburbia. The homes here weren't as broken as some I'd passed, but there were a few well on their way. There was an overflowing box of empty beer cans in the road as I approached 77.

There were two cars in the driveway, an old Ford pickup truck and a newer minivan. I could see an elevated playhouse for children in the back yard. There was minor landscaping, the grass was cut, and the house didn't need paint. The lights were on, and I could see the glow of that great God of living rooms. It was as average as average gets. I moved on, went to 92.

It was as different from 77 as it could get without sticking out. One car, newer Ford with a quad cab. Grass looked swept, not mowed, almost as if the wind had bent it. I knew what that really meant; lawn mower had a bad blade. I walked past the driveway, staying in the street. Watching. There was at least one dog, big one too. There were droppings in the front yard but more in the back—I could see them through the chain-link fence. No Beware of Dog sign, no post or dog run. Guard dog. Two sheds in the back yard, both in the same level of disrepair as the house and yard. I could practically hear Shelby yelling for help. I wandered a little further on the side, not in the lawn but close. The feeling of being watched increased. I knelt, pretending to tie a shoe.

I walked from the house a little further down the street and saw what I was looking for. House with a sign on the door, realtor listing in the yard. I gave a look and slipped through the side yard between houses. They backed up to another row of houses, but there was a ridge of trees between the two. I stayed close to the trees and made my way to 92. If I was being watched, I hadn't noticed.

I poked my head through the trees and went through to the other side of them. I knew when I was there. I knelt and stuck myself between a pair of massive pines, finally got a good look at the yard.

The grass in front had been ill cared for, but in back it was just gone. The sheds framed in the corners, maybe twenty-five feet apart, painted a matching black. On the back of the house a sign said, "Trespassers will be shot." There was nothing to tell me Shelby was in the house or either of the sheds, but there was nothing to indicate that she wasn't, either. I'd need to be thorough, go in the house, check the sheds. I'd need help. Arrow.

I left, went back to the bike. I'd seen all I could see in the light, and it was time to go. I rode home as fast as I could. I walked in, took the burner out of my pocket, and called her. I was breaking one of my laws.

"Hey. Don't talk, all right? Can you skip school tomorrow?"

"Yes. Why?"

"No. Meet me at the gas station just outside of Four Oaks at nine a.m. Dress to move; bring your bike and a backpack."

"Anything else?"

Bring two revolvers, help me catch the bad guys and find your sister alive, and then marry me. We'll move to the coast and live like royalty. I'll have a dog, and eventually we'll have two kids, a boy and a girl. You can name them whatever you want. We'll die together after a long and wonderful life.

"Yes. Tomorrow could be bad. Can you deal with that?"

Silence. Then solid: "Yes."

She hung up. I replaced the phone in the cradle and brought my go-chest to my filthy kitchen table. When this was all done, I was cleaning and going shopping. If I could.

I laid the war chest, my get-out-of-town box, on the ground and opened it. I emptied my pockets on the table, took the starting pistol from my waist, and closed my eyes. Opened them. Built a kit. Hoped it was good enough. Knew it might not be. I accepted that. Arrow shouldn't be involved. There was no way for her not be. When I was all ready to go, I went to bed. Lay there, thinking about rundown houses in neighborhoods that had run off the tracks. Thought about Shelby—to me, just a picture, to Arrow, her little sister, to her parents, a lifeline back to normalcy. Thought about going to war. If Shelby was there and I couldn't get her out, I wasn't going anywhere either. Endless thoughts boiling my brain in cruel waters. I didn't sleep well.

Chapter 33

Arrow met me just like I knew she would, and I handed her the bag with the ghillie suit and mask, an unused burner, and spotting scope in it. Two pictures, as clear as I could get my printer to make them, of Henry and Fred. She looked in the bag, shifted things around, and said, "What's all this for?"

"So you can tell me when he shows up to work."

"I'm going with you."

"No. I need you in the woods so I can be sure it will be safe to break into his house. I need to know if he leaves so I can be out of the house. I need you here much more than I need you there, alright?"

"I don't like it."

"You don't have to like it, but I need you to do this and stop arguing with me about it, alright?"

"Okay."

She looked at me, eyes wet and full of hope. "Do you think she's there?"

"I don't know. I just know he's part of it."

"Okay."

She looked better having heard that. I wish it had been true, but thinking something might be and knowing it were a far distance apart.

"When you see them, verify faces and nametags. I wrote their names on the pictures of their heads. Be sure. If it's not them, we'll try again tomorrow. They were here yesterday though, and I think they'll be on the same job today. We just have to hope for the best. Make sure you use the burner to call me; the number for my phone is written on tape on the back of yours."

"Okay."

I got on my bike, and I didn't look back. I just rode, tried not to think about the lack of a Beware of Dog sign or the police arresting me for breaking into the home of a man guilty of nothing more than living by a friend and not keeping up on his yard. I thought about what I had to do and how it would play out in the limitless ways this thing could go. My life was about control, thinking three or four steps ahead so I could never fall behind. Today I was jumping headfirst into the zero, into the unknown. If I was smart and stuck to what I knew, everything should be fine. Tell that to Shelby.

The houses and yards did their little magic trick again, and around me the world bloomed into subservience, children went to school, adults went to work. They did what they were told, kept their noses clean. Civilians, nothing wrong with it, but if they only knew that they could choose, is that what they would have picked? Would they pay taxes, work for a system that could discard them like yesterday's trash? The collapse of the auto industry should have been a heads-up—good guys can lose when rich men play with money. If it was a sign, nobody saw it.

I parked my bike at the opposite end of Duiker from the night before and walked back to the house with the realtor listing in the yard. I felt like I was walking on the African savannah, a stranger surrounded by strange things. I just hoped I'd see the lion before he saw me. I crept between the houses, and being as careful as I could, I slowly moved to 92 Duiker. There hadn't been a car in the driveway when I came by, but that didn't mean anything. I sat in the trees, arms wrapped around myself with the burner shaking in my hands. When it rang a half hour later, I almost screamed.

"He's here."

"The other one?"

"No. Not yet."

"Call me."

I hung up and stuck the phone in my pocket. Opened my backpack. Took out the length of two-by-four and the steak I'd injected with Ketamine. The kids call it Special K; veterinarians call it a horse tranquilizer. I closed the backpack, tossed it over my shoulder, and gripped the board in one hand, the steak in the other. I hopped the chain-link fence and looked in both directions. Trees in yards broke up my lines; it would take someone actively looking to see me, and I had a feeling people around here were used to not looking at this yard. I took the board, grabbed my lungs a deep breath of the good stuff, and shattered the window out of the back door. I tossed in the steak just as the barking started. I sat on the stoop and waited. The barking stopped. I craned my arm in through the shattered window and turned the knob. I took a deep breath, steeled myself, and held the wood in front of me like a shield. The door swung open, and I went inside.

Chapter 34

The pit bull forgot the steak as soon as it saw me. It must have had some training. If it were my dog, I would have taught it not to eat food from a stranger. I knew two things going in. Rhino had taught me to always fight a stronger force by using that force to exploit its own expectations, to set a trap, and he'd taught me to use leverage—that was all jiu-jitsu was. Use his leverage and bend him. It jumped at my throat, and I shoved the board in its mouth. Big dogs expect you to pull away from a bite, to back up and look for space. That's how they kill you. I drove the board into its mouth, tried to get a look at the steak as I brought Fido to the ground. Two big chunks were missing from the meat. I had to hope it was enough. I held the dog with the board as it struggled and then weakened beneath me before falling on her side. She had scars on her back. It must have taken a big, brave man to beat her enough to make those show through the dog's fur. I watched her fall into a slumber on the tile floor, and when I was sure she was down, I got to work.

The house was the polar opposite of the yard. It must have driven him half nuts to have the outside of his home look like that. The inside reeked of money and Pine-Sol. I left the dog and the kitchen and went to look.

Typical little one-story house, the front room camouflaged like the outside had been, ratty TV, nasty carpet, a few beer cans lying around. The door that led to it in the kitchen was painted white and was very clean. The side that faced the living room was filthy.

I walked through the crummy parlor. The blinds were pulled tight, and there were three types of locking systems on the front door. I walked past it and went through the other filthy door. It led to a bedroom with an attached bath, both as immaculate as the kitchen had been. I checked the closet—just clothes. So far, I was failing. The front room was proof that something was going on, but not of what.

I went back to the kitchen and the sleeping dog. Opened all the cupboards, found nothing but dust, three jars of peanut butter, and some canned corn. Opened the fridge and found a pack of hot dogs, tub of margarine, jar of jelly, and a two weeks expired bottle of milk. There were two loaves of white bread on the counter, but that was it for food. I gave the dog a look; she was one passed-out puppy. I felt bad for needing to drug her. I like dogs.

There was a closet across from the fridge. I opened it. This was where all the food was. There were boxes of macaroni, packages of ramen noodles, cans of every which thing, ravioli, okra, potatoes, boxes and boxes of cereal. Packages of fruit roll-ups, fruit snacks, crackers, chips, and pudding cups. Piles upon piles of comestibles, really a little grocery store—I have to admit, I got some hunger pangs just looking. I stepped back to close the door, thought better of it, and cleared off the top shelf of breakfast cereal, just knocked it all on the floor. Everything was still packaged like they'd just made a Costco run—the pudding was in fours, the chili was in a six-pack string, and the cereal boxes were unopened. Picked up the shelf the food sat on and knocked on the paneling behind it. Nothing there. Hollow.

I cleared the rest of the shelves off as quickly as I was able to. It looked like there'd been a fight in a grocery store by the time I was done. This had to be a serious pain for these guys every time they wanted to go downstairs. I pulled the remaining boards from the closet one after another. They were loose, made to be removed like this in a hurry. When they were all out, I knocked again on the paneling, harder now that I was closer. The whole thing was hollow. I pressed my hands against it and tried to slide it. Nothing. I tried the other way. Resistance, but there was something there. I stepped back to look at the wood, see if there was a keyhole or something I was missing. I stepped in and tried again, lifting up this time as I pushed to the right.

My momentum slid me into the wall with the door as it shook free. I was met by a top step and nothing else. The stench from the basement was nearly unbearable. It was utterly putrid, like rotten fruits and meats had been left to molder with one another. Just as unsettling was that until I'd moved the board, there'd been no smell at all. There was no light switch or pull chain visible. I took the flashlight from my pocket and went into the darkness.

Chapter 35

The steps were rickety, scary enough on their own, really, even if there had been light. But they were backless, too, indefensible—if someone were under them, they could have gotten to the backs of my legs, and there was nothing I could do about it. I could all but feel a hand gripping my ankle or slicing my Achilles tendon, sending me swirling into the black, the door above slamming behind me. I kept my legs ready to pounce, to leap away from danger, though in the back of my head I knew that would be impossible. Once I got down there, my assailant would also know the room and would probably be armed. I just had to hope that whatever secrets the basement held, one of them wasn't an enemy.

The stench grew as I lowered myself into the cavern, and it took a conscious effort to keep my free hand at the ready instead of covering my mouth and nose. As I descended, I saw that in addition to being boards with no backs, the steps entered the basement at its center, defying the logic of the floor plan of the upstairs. This house probably hadn't been built by a kidnapper or a murderer, but it might as well have been.

I walked into hell.

When I reached the bottom of the steps, I saw a corpse. Just off to one side, among some boxes and suitcases, was a man with a bullet hole in the center of his head. There was no reason to check his pulse; he was too bloated to even tell his ethnicity. I stayed away from the corpse as best I was able and tried my hardest to keep my other hand away from my face to keep it ready to strike or grab. Then I turned past a high stack of boxes that separated the stairs from the rest of the room—and I saw her.

Shelby or not, she was dead.

The girl was bound to the chair with ratcheting straps, like what you'd use to hold something on a trailer. Her mouth was covered in duct tape, her hair drooped and dirty next to her head. She was naked save for a pair of underwear and a filthy tank top. I grabbed her forehead to tilt her face up, to know. The hair was just too dirty. I lifted her up, stared at her face. She was like a mini, wasted version of Arrow. It was Shelby. I let the light go over her face. Her eyes popped open, and I fell backwards.

She thrashed against the chair, bouncing as hard as she could, but it was bolted to the floor. Hurt and malnourished, but she still wanted to fight.

"Stop," I said. "Arrow sent me. Calm down, I'm here to help."

She stopped immediately, looked in my eyes.

I looked back, said, "Trust me."

I took the lock-blade out of my backpack, opened it, and got to work sawing at her bonds. The first went easy, but the rest were dulling the edge of my knife. I started to go upstairs to see about a kitchen knife, but her eyes stopped me. They said, "Don't leave me alone." I took the tape off of her face and got back to work. I knelt next to a stain that had to be blood and started cutting through the straps that bound her wrists. She spoke, her voice raspy and thick, every word a struggle.

"Who are you?"

"I'm Nickel."

I finished a leg, and she kicked it free, testing to see if it still worked. I couldn't blame her.

"Your sister hired me to find you. Sorry it took so long."

Somehow, even after everything that had happened, she still had the capacity to be surprised. I could see the light in her eyes twinkle for a lost moment as she spoke. "You're just a kid, like me."

"Yep."

I got the other ankle free and then got to work on her wrist.

"Aren't the cops looking for me?"

"They think your dad did it."

"Kidnapped me?"

"Killed you."

I cut the wrist free; two straps to go.

"Is he in jail?"

"Yes."

"He must be so angry!"

I thought about that as I cut. I imagined that would be the case. I got the strap from her waist free. Just one left, the one that bound her neck to a board affixed to the chair.

She said, "I'm so thirsty."

"I bet. I'll have you loose soon."

I looked around the room and saw a business card taped to one of the cement walls behind her. I stood and said, "Hold on."

The card was held onto the wall with masking tape. All it had on it was a phone number. I stuck it in my pocket and got back to work cutting.

The knife was fighting the coarse fabric of the strap; my teeth were clenched with the effort of cutting and not pulling on it so far as to choke her. She'd been through enough—she didn't need me strangling her. I felt something vibrate on my leg. I took the burner out and answered it.

"Nickel?"

"What?"

"They're gone!"

"What?"

"They're gone, five, maybe six minutes ago! I've been calling, but I couldn't get a signal in the woods!"

I hung up, dropped the phone, and began sawing furiously at the last strap. The knife was only biting on every other slice; I was hacking furiously, trying to ignore the choked sounds coming from Shelby. Finally, she was free. I threw the backpack on, pushed the knife in my pocket with the blade still open, and grabbed the phone in one hand and Shelby's wrist in the other. I pulled, almost dragged her up the stairs. My ears begged not to hear the front door open.

I ran and she limped past the dog and scattered groceries and out the back door. I dropped the backpack, tore off my sweatshirt, and handed it to her; it went down just onto her thighs. I helped her over the fence and climbed over it myself. Heard a diesel motor, a truck, somewhere in the distance. Grabbed her wrist, and we ran, probably the motliest-looking pair ever. I had my burner to my ear, calling Lou.

"Pick up, pick up."

"This is Lou."

"I need you. Now."

"Where."

"I'm on Duiker right now. We're going to be heading west on my bicycle, two of us, one bike. At least two bad guys."

"Riverside?"

"Sure."

We made my bike. I tossed the phone in my pocket and ripped the bike free from the chain and left it behind. I could get new iron. I mounted the bike and helped Shelby on in front of me so she could use the seat. I put my arms around her and started pedaling. Behind us, I could hear a truck. A big one.

Chapter 36

We had maybe a mile head start on them. Without Shelby I could have turned off and gotten away, but I wasn't going to leave her. We'd die together if we had to. We cut down cross-streets and that motor would dull, and then it would be right behind us again, not there, but close. Closer all the time. Riverside was almost a mile out. I pushed, found a rhythm, made the bike heave against the wind, feeling iron and diesel smoke at my back. Not caring. Caring about the little girl passing out on the seat in front of me. Feeling her heartbeat against my chest and telling myself over and over again that if we were going to die, they were coming with us. Telling myself to remember my training, telling myself to fight.

I turned my head back when we were less than two blocks from the park. They were following us slowly, right on my tail. I slowed and then stood on the pedals, riding on the sidewalk, hoping for a crowd in the park. They were right next to us, the one in the passenger seat rolling the window down, waving a steel revolver. I kept my right hand on the bicycle handle, prayed Shelby wouldn't fall to the left, and pulled my starting pistol with my free arm. The truck broke hard to the left, and I fired three blanks at it. They backed off, and I put the gun hand on the left pedal. The bike bounced over a short hill in the sidewalk and hit lawn. We were there. All we had to do was cross the park; Lou and his cab would be waiting. May as well have been across the Atlantic.

I dropped the bicycle and helped shake Shelby free of the frame. The truck was idling at the edge of the park, and they were getting out just as we'd gotten free of the bike. They were coming for us, and there was no one here to stop them. I felt Shelby tugging at my arm, dragging me back. I pulled her around a thick maple, and we headed towards the playground, to my old meeting spot. All of this crap, all of the secrets, the being careful, everything gone wrong because of crap reception on a stupid burner. We were almost to the playground when I dropped the bag and pulled out the can of butane. I opened it, scratched a match across my belt buckle, lit the top of the can with the match, and threw it in their direction. The explosion was green and slowed them. The one with the revolver raised it, and I dragged Shelby to the ground with me, bullets tugging the air over us.

I stood, still holding onto Shelby. We were almost to the playground, halfway to the parking lot. We ran, bullets in the air around us—too far for a pistol unless they got lucky. I zipped past the monkey bars and the jungle gyms, rounded the pond. Eyepatch was standing. I stopped. Shelby tugged at my arm, screaming. Eyepatch walked past us toward them, pulling an enormous pistol from his coat, kept moving and started throwing lead. He held up his free hand, firing with the other one. One of the men went down. Eyepatch shook his hand at us, almost like he was waving with the extended arm. The pistol bucked. Someone was screaming in the park besides Shelby. We ran.

Chapter 37

Lou was sitting in his cab, waiting. He raised his eyebrows when he saw us. Big reaction. I pulled the backpack off and helped Shelby in. I felt lightheaded, looked at my arm—bleeding, a hole in my shirt. Crimson soaking my side and Lou's unfortunate seat. I leaned against Shelby, trying to get my strength back.

"Where to?"

"Take me to Rhino's. She needs to go to the hospital after you drop me off. Shelby, you need to forget that you saw me today. Can you do that?"

She was falling asleep. I shook her twice. She looked at me, not all there. I smacked her across the face. She focused in, held her cheek.

"Shelby. You didn't see me today, okay? Arrow knows how to get hold of me. You were being held at 92 Duiker Road by two men named Hank and Fred, and you escaped on your own. Make up whatever you want to say, but stick to what you say the first time."

She looked at Lou. "What about him?"

"Lou knows how to keep his mouth shut."

We were getting close to Rhino's. I could feel the world fading on me. I shook my head. Shook it again, tried to bounce back.

146

I opened the backpack and pulled out my wallet. It was stuffed with hundreds. I tossed them through the little window dividing the cab.

"Is that enough?"

Lou looked down, then looked back at me. He used whatever internal calculator he was born with that processed a fair price for the transport of two youths. Both of whom the police would desperately want to talk to, and one of whom was ruining the back seat of his cab. He nodded.

"If it's not, you know where to find me."

He grunted. The guy was really talkative today. He pulled into the lot in front of Rhino's gym, and I grabbed the bag and got out. I stood by the open door, wavering for a second. I locked eyes with Shelby.

"Remember what I said."

She nodded and gave me a little smile. Girl was as beautiful as her older sister. I walked from the car, made it through the entryway into the gym, and the world went black.

Chapter 38

I woke in Rhino's office. I recognized the posters and awards that littered the walls. A man I didn't know sat next to me, and it all started coming back. The man talked with a thick East Coast accent; I could practically smell the Jersey sewage. "He's awake."

Rhino's face appeared above my own. "Hey, he's awake! What trouble you in now?"

"You don't want to know."

"Young and smart. Rare."

Rhino nodded at the doctor, and the man spoke. He was a wispy little thing, and his hat was covered in little ribbons, badges, and pins. "Your stitches need to come out in a week. You know how to take them out?"

I nodded. I could've put them in if I'd been awake.

"You got lucky, kid, really lucky."

He had no idea.

"Guy shot you with a full metal jacket, bang, but it's a bullet that don't expand. He gets you with a hollow point, you lose the arm right where he shot you. Fall over, bleed out. Dead. The full metal, he needs an organ or piece in your skull to put you down for good." He shook his head, disgusted. "This crap with the guns, it's no good—you kids should know better. Used to be you had a problem, you just settled it with your fists. Now it's all guns and gangs. If Rhino hadn't made me fix you, I would've sent your butt to the hospital, let you talk to the cops. Do ya some good."

Rhino had his hands on his knees, laughing as hard as he was able. He said, "No, Stitch, this boy, he okay, he is my friend. This is Nickel—you no heard of Nickel?"

Stitch withdrew and dropped back like he was choking. "He's young."

"He's a good boy, good friend. You need problem solved, this is the man for the job."

I said, "It'll be on the house."

Rhino clapped his enormous hands together. "You feeling better already!"

Stitch was packing things back into a ring bag.

"How long have I been here?"

"Two days. You woke up once, yelled for a girl. Shelby or Sadie I think. I make Stitch give you morphine. Powerful!"

I watched Stitch leave the room. As he closed the door, I said, "Thank you."

"I'm gonna call in that marker kid, don't forget."

"I won't."

The door closed behind him. It was just Rhino and me. He threw me a shirt. I caught it with my good arm, gave the stitches and their surrounding bruise a look, and pulled it over my head. My wounded arm burned as I yanked the shirt over the injury. I felt woozy and had to concentrate to clear my head.

Rhino said, "You okay?"

"Yeah. Just banged up."

He lifted my backpack from behind his desk and set it on the cot next to me. "You come in, you were a mess."

I nodded.

"You are a very lucky boy."

"I know."

He took something off of his desk, folded it, and handed it over. It was a newspaper. "I give you a few minutes, get your head right."

Rhino sat behind his desk and picked up a book. I looked at the headline. "Two Killed in Kidnapping Escape!" I went to the meat. My hands shook a little as I folded the paper and read.

Suspected kidnappers Henry "Hank" Phillips and Freddy Jefferson were both shot dead at the scene of a Tuesday afternoon gunfight in Riverside Park. The man who shot them was detained by authorities and released.

A police source confirmed that both Phillips and Johnson were discharging handguns and chasing a young girl they'd kidnapped and were holding captive at their house when the third gunman opened fire and killed both of them.

It has not been confirmed whether the third shooter was legally armed or not, but Police Sergeant Bill Van Endel said, "We are happy that the young lady has been returned to her parents and that someone was able to come to her aid in a time of great need."

The girl is believed to be Shelby Cross, missing since last week. Her father, Adam Cross, has been released from police custody in light of the recent events.

It went on, had some quotes from an NRA spokesperson about how citizens needed to be their own last line of defense. I hadn't seen anything insinuating that an attractive young hero had been present, or an ugly red-headed boy for that matter, so Shelby had done well, and Eyepatch and Lou knew enough to keep quiet too. It's possible they were looking for someone fitting my description, but the only risk there would be them discovering that I kept to myself and probably ought to go back to foster care. I read the article again. If they were looking for me, it was on the low. I stood and set the paper on Rhino's desk.

"Would you mind having someone call me a cab?"

Rhino smiled and said, "You don't need a cab. Your friend Jeff, he can give you a ride."

Rhino peeled ten hundred-dollar bills out of his desk and laid them in front of me. I looked at the money, considered it, and swept into a fold that I tucked in my pocket.

"Your finder's fee. He a fighter. A real fighter."

Rhino stood and walked to the door. He opened it and extended an arm. I followed him out.

Jeff was working a heavy bag that had been taken off of its chain and laid on its side on some wrestling mats. He was kneeling on one side of it, and then with lightning speed he would throw a punch at the top of the bag, toss a leg over it, fire punches from the mounted position, and then pop to the other side to repeat it. We watched him work through the routine, and when Jeff started to slow, Rhino clapped his hands to let him know we were watching.

Jeff stood and walked towards us, bowing deeply before Rhino. Rhino bowed back, not quite as deep, and said, "You remember your friend Nickel?"

"Of course I do. How are you, Nickel?"

Rhino cut me off. "He's good, but needs a favor. Can you give him a ride?"

Jeff grabbed a towel off of a rack and dried his face. "Sure. Right now?"

Rhino nodded.

Jeff slipped into a pair of flip-flops and said, "Let's go."

Chapter 39

We left in the car I'd seen Jeff pull into the field at Knapps. I sat quietly while Jeff drove. When we were almost to my house, I pointed to a gas station and said, "Just let me off there."

"I don't mind driving you home…"

"No, this is good. Thank you."

Jeff flicked the button to unlock the doors and said, "I wanted to thank you. The last few days have been the best of my whole life."

I thought about running through the field with Shelby, bullets in the air around us. Thought about fires and Nick and Eleanor. I pushed the ugliness out of my head. I tried to think just about Jeff, about where his life had been and where it was going now.

"You're welcome. Rhino thinks you'll be a fighter."

Jeff nodded, gravely.

"When you get a fight, have Rhino find me. I want to see what you can do with some training. You were good when you were rough, but Rhino will make you a force. He builds weapons."

"If you ever need anything—anything—you let me know, and I will come, no questions asked."

"I will."

He extended his hand, and I gave him mine. I could feel his pulse through his palm as he shook my much smaller hand.

"I'm serious. I don't know anything about you; Rhino wouldn't tell me a thing. But I can look at you and know that something scared you bad recently. If I can help…"

"Then I'll let you know. You read the paper?"

"Sometimes. Why?"

"Ask Rhino for the copy in his office. Read between the lines. Make sure you want to get involved with me. I know I'm just a kid, but that's a big offer, and I want you to know what you're getting involved with if we work together. Thanks for the ride."

I got out and waited until he drove off. I walked home. It was hard, but not as awful as I'd expected it to be. For the first time since I'd moved in, I wanted to see a neighbor, just some reminder of humanity. Opened the garage door. Missed my bike. Went inside and slept like a rock.

Chapter 40

When I woke, it was night. I was cold. No covers. If there'd been dreams, they were gone. I got up. Gave up, went back, and lay in the blackness. I've never felt so alone. After enough time, I slept.

When I woke again, it was light. I checked my pager. Nothing. I went to the computer, looked at my bank account—not too shabby right now, just under seventy thou. I went bike shopping, found my old model, a Gary Fisher Roscoe 3, ordered that and some Dura-Coat to paint it. Matte black, just like the last time. If there's a better bike, I want to know about it; right now that's as good as it gets. There are people who will tell you that mountain bikes are no good for street, and they're kind of right. The thing is, though, no road bike is any good at the rough stuff. I need one that can do both. I left the computer and grabbed a book off the shelf, *Blue Belle* by Vachss. Went outside, watered the garden. Read for a while.

I'd promised myself that if I lived through getting Shelby, I'd clean the house and go shopping, get some real food. Now those were the last things in the world that I cared about. I shut the water off and tried to pretend I was reading. All I could think about was Arrow and Shelby—and how I was never going to see them again.

It was the worst part about my work, when I'd really connected with a case and just put everything into it. I tried to ball up that thinking, just get it gone. Tried to roll a scheme to move that money, but I was drawing blanks. Put all that crap aside. My pot needed some work done, I had stuff to live for, and I had stuff that needed doing. It wasn't my fault that none of it mattered. I went to the garden and got to it. When I was done, I had a tote full of trimmings to hang. This sucks on a normal day, and my hurt arm made it even worse. I took the cut plants to the basement and flittered around there for a bit. When hunger came, she bit hard. I went upstairs and ordered some sandwiches from a pizza joint. I cleaned the table, put my get-out-of-town box away, and put the tools and camera equipment and all the other stuff away too. Went back to the basement, started laundry. The light hooked to the doorbell flashed while I was down there.

I paid the kid with a twenty and told him to keep the rest, just like a spoiled little brat home alone would. He never even thought about me. I was voracious with the food; I'd ordered a meatball sub and a club, and I hate half of each. I put what was left in the fridge and sat on the couch. Checked my pager. Nothing. Ran to the washer. Remembered something that was hopefully still legible. The card.

I was lucky—I'd thrown it on top of the washer when I checked my pockets. I never check my pockets. Never. I read the number, plugged in line six, and dialed. Got that fail noise and then the "this number has been disconnected" bit. I hung up, cleared the line. I'd read about this. I went to the computer.

I was pretty sure I'd read on a pedo board about a year or so ago that one of the new tricks in the game was to set up a contact number that ran a disconnected or call failed message. Only what that message really is, is a lobby. You know, like when you call customer support, and a recorded voice starts asking for codes and addresses? "Press one for English," that kind of stuff. This was the same thing.

It doesn't matter what those messages say, it's how you respond. The gas company wants you to pay your bill, so they don't have automated systems that make it harder than necessary to do so. But if you wanted to make it so that it was impossible to use a number unless you used a code, then you'd set up a system like this. The one I read about had a lockout. You fail once on a line, the line is dead to the system—that disconnected message becomes real. I ran upstairs to my computer and tried to find mention of a coded system on the perv forums but got nothing. I left the office and went outside.

I needed to call Arrow, but it was the last thing in the world I wanted to do. There were just too many possible rejections there, and I didn't see myself dealing well with any of them. But if Shelby had overheard anything about their plans for her, she might be able to give me some idea of what to do. I couldn't imagine Shelby was up to talking—I was sure she was still hospitalized, or if not hospitalized surely spending a lot of time talking, between the head-shrinkers and detectives. I stared off for a little while, just letting it all come together in my head. Finally broke. I grabbed a jacket and walked to a pay phone to call Arrow.

It was getting cold out, winter sending out tendrils of its coming storm. Winter doesn't bother me, and neither do summer or spring. Fall weather, though, weather like this, I hate it. If spring is birth, summer is life, and winter is death, then the fall is dying. The world fades around you, exploding with red and orange colors before wasting to nothing. The snow I can deal with, but watching the world around me die and get swept up terrifies me in ways that I can't explain. Maybe it's a fear that spring will never come, that things will just be desolate forever. The world acts so insulated, so sure that there will be a spring, that life will be warm and good. Go to any city, find a women's shelter. Ask around about that. You'll get blank eyes and broken hearts. Go deeper, find a center for children recovering from sexual abuse. Ask those children if they think everything will ever be okay again. I already know the answer. Want to guess?

I walked to the gas station by Arrow's house before calling. I'm stubborn like that sometimes. She answered, and I said, "Can you talk?"

"Nic…yes. When?"

"Now, I'm at the gas station."

"Alright. I'll be there in a few minutes."

I hung up and thought about leaving. What if the police were watching the house? I decided it was worth the risk to see her. I sat on the curb by the phone and drew my sweatshirt around me. I was staring at the ground and didn't even hear her roll up to me. All I knew was that one second I was sitting, and the next I was getting tackled. I lifted my head up, hoping that it would be Arrow who had done the tackling, and I was pleased to see through a shock of red-tinged blonde hair that it was. I put my elbow down to lift myself up, and she stood and wrapped her bike chain like I'd taught her. She turned to me when she was finished with tears in her eyes and said, "Nickel, thank you so much. You saved her. You saved Shelby."

She wrapped me in a hug, and I could feel the fire in my cheeks. I wanted to push her back, say something cool like, "All in a day's work, babe," and then stick a matchstick in my mouth and just fire off questions. Instead I just let her hold me. When she let me go, it was far too soon. I could feel her heat come off of me like a veil. She was smiling; I gave her one back—a real one. It felt good. I said, "Let's go for a walk."

"The park?"

"Too soon."

"We tried to get your bike back, but the cops took it. They don't believe Shelby."

"About what?"

"About her being alone. They won't tell us why they don't believe her, but one of them said something about straps being cut. Did you have to cut her free?"

"Yeah. She was strapped pretty tight to a chair."

"I think they figure there was a third guy in the kidnapping that got cold feet and decided to let her go. Did you know they found a body in the house? They left it out of the paper as a secret, so if another person does come forward they can tell if they're lying or not. Shelby told them that they killed him in front of her, said that they'd kill her too if she tried to get away. She told them she woke up and she was free, and she just ran."

"Did Eyepatch say anything?"

"All I heard was that he told the cops that he saw two men shooting at a little girl, and that wouldn't stand in his park. You know Eyepatch sits there like a guardian? The cops told us he's been waiting for this to happen every day. It's like he knew you guys would need help."

She was right, he had known. Not for what or when, but eventually. He'd been right. Luckily for us.

Eyepatch had been a curiosity before, just "the man who would not wave," but now that I knew a little bit, I wanted to know everything about him, like if the lawyer story was true, and if he'd ever done anything like that before. And why hadn't he ever scared me? I'd never even felt slightly odd about what he chose to do with his time. There wasn't an adult in the world who didn't make me at least a little wary, but with Eyepatch, nothing. Was there some internal survivor radar or something in me that could let me detect people who'd been through things like me?

"How's Shelby?"

"She's okay. They didn't do…anything to her."

"Does she know why they took her?"

"The cops think they were going to sell her and were holding out for more money. The guy who lived at that house, Hank, he's been doing this for years. I guess they've been looking for him forever. If I hadn't called you…"

She didn't need to finish it. We both knew: Shelby would be gone, maybe dead, certainly wishing she was if she weren't.

"Can you talk to Shelby for me?"

"About what?"

I told her about the card and the loaded number, about needing a password. I told her it wasn't over for me, not yet. I didn't tell her how dirty it was going to get.

"What should I say?"

"Ask if she heard them talking on the phone, and if she did, ask if they would start off conversations with a code word. If they were using keys to punch a number in, then this is done, we'll never find them. If they were verbally being allowed into the system, then maybe I can work some magic and get a meet."

"I'll ask her. It's hard, though—there's always somebody around."

"Just do your best. How are your parents?"

"They're okay. My mom laid off the booze, at least for a while, and my dad's been sleeping on the couch. He apologized to me, but I'm still angry with him for cheating on my mom. I'm never going to be like that when I grow up. No matter what."

I believed her.

"Tell Shelby that I'm glad to hear she's doing okay."

"Nickel, she says you're the bravest person she's ever met in her life. You saved her. She says you weren't even scared when they were shooting at you guys. She can't wait to thank you in person."

"She's wrong. I was terrified."

"It doesn't matter." She gave me another hug, shorter than the last. Kissed me on the cheek, an explosion. "I'll talk to her and I'll call you, tonight probably. Don't be a stranger—just because it's not work doesn't mean we can't be friends."

"I know. I will."

We were back at the gas station. I watched her unwrap her bike and mount it. Watched her ride off, blonde and fire-streaked hair in the wind behind her. Beautiful Arrow. When she was gone I left, colder than I'd been before. Cold to the bone.

I stopped on the way home, bought some breakfast cereal. I ate three bowls of Captain Crunch when I got back to the house— after, the roof of my mouth felt like I'd been chewing nails. I was washing the bowl and loading the dishwasher when my pager buzzed. I rinsed my hand and read it. Arrow. I dried off with a towel and called her back.

"Here's the short version."

"Alright."

"They always said bark. Like on a tree."

"Alright."

I hung up. I knew she'd understand. I finished loading the dishwasher, but my heart wasn't in it. When I was done, I put my jacket back on and walked to the gas station. Man, I miss my bike—everything takes so much longer without it. I took the business card from my pocket and considered it. Put two thick breath mints in my mouth and picked up the receiver. Dropped two quarters in the slot and dialed. The little spiel started, and I said, "Bark."

The spiel stopped. A few seconds later a man answered. "Can I help you?"

"I got your number from an acquaintance. He said you can get things."

"I am in the business, but the nature of supply and demand can make such work difficult. What are you looking to acquire?"

"A girl. White, between seven and ten years old. Not too big."

"That's pretty specific. You know these things can be expensive?"

"Yes. Money is not an issue. I also have something that might interest you."

"Oh?"

"A boy. Twelve years old. He's conditioned."

"Very interesting. For the girl, two hundred and fifty thou sand dollars. Flat, cash, obviously. I make no guarantees of the hardiness of my stock. You play at your own risk."

I could not wait to meet this guy. My hands were shaking. "What do I get for the boy?"

"If he's clean, between fifty and a hundred."

"When can I make a play on the merchandise?"

"I'll need to be sure of inventory. Call me tomorrow, this number, same time."

Before I could respond, he'd hung up. I wasn't scared; I was too busy making a plan. The wheels were spinning faster and faster, but I wasn't missing a thing. I walked home. I wasn't cold now; I had work to do. I was ready to get back into combat.

Chapter 41

Before I built the fake electrical box at the school, I put a similar one in a yard about a block from my house. I've used it a couple of times, but it sits empty most of the time. The couple who lives there has done some really nice landscaping around it, which is all the more impressive because they can't even really see it unless they're outside. It's not as nice as the one I built for the school, but it was my first try and it's held up really well, especially considering the weather. I called the woman with the money.

"Hello?"

"It's a friend."

"Okay…"

"I can make it work, but I need the merch clean. No deposit either."

"Not possible."

"I am not putting good money towards bad. Put feelers out; is there anyone in this state that would give real tender for scratch? I know you don't want to mess with Chicago, or you'd already be there. You came to me for a reason—the normal channels weren't getting the results you wanted, and you want to see if I can pass phonies to a bunch of kids, make the money look like it's coming from everywhere. I can make a flood, make it so you can put some fake bucks into whatever your real plan is, but you need to trust me."

Silence. She took a break. I was good with that, and I waited.

"Where's the drop?"

I gave her an address, instructions, told her about the other box. She didn't laugh, just tucked it in tight. I thought we were done when she said, "You know, if you do me wrong on this, it's going to be a mess."

"Lady, I don't know what you heard about me, but this won't go sour because of me. Put it this way: I know I'm not playing, and so do you. I don't need to pull a scam for the same reason that I don't need this job in the first place. This is about making a little by being careful, not trying to score on some ugly bucks and messing up my name."

It must have reassured her, or maybe she was just sick of hearing my gums flap, because when I stopped talking she was gone. I unplugged my phone and leaned back in the chair. Waited around the house and killed time for a couple of hours. Went to the garage, got the little cart I bought for gardening, and went for a walk. I know in movies, money changes hands in nice-looking attaché cases. That's nice for a small chunk of change, I guess, but when you're doing money like this, you need space. I checked the box after I was sure no one was watching. Tightly wrapped parcels of saran wrap, bound thick with packing tape. She either didn't trust the ink, or didn't trust me to get the money today. With counterfeiters, the problem is either the product or greed; usually the both wrapped up together made for a messy little package. She better hope this money looked as good as that first hundred she showed me, or this was going to go over poorly.

I wheeled it home and trucked it in the house, took the wraps off, and gave it a look. Not bad—not real, but it would work. If I lived, she'd get paid, I'd get paid, and some nasty people would go to where they needed to be that much faster. I went to my room and lay down. I slept better than I thought I would.

Chapter 42

I spent most of the day just trying not to think about what I had to do. There was a solid little plan in my head, but making it all work would take some effort. It sat in my subconscious the way things like that always do. You can't make yourself not think about something. The UPS man interrupted my bad thoughts and sharpened my day, one big package and one little one—my bike had arrived! If he thought it was weird that I was home from school, he didn't show it. I dragged the thing to the garage, opened up the box holding my beautiful bike, and got to making it look less pretty.

The first thing was to take it apart. The first time I did it I was nervous I'd lose a part or bend something I wasn't supposed to. I'm not nervous about anything like that anymore. I turned on the little stereo I keep out there, turned it up loud. Dillinger Four, *Midwestern Songs of the Americas*. Album's older than I am, but it's perfect. I sang along while I broke down the bike and hung it in pieces from the rafters. I used coat hangers instead of string. When the bike was stripped and spread across the garage, I hooked up my airbrush gun and turned on the compressor. I could feel the thrum of the vibrations in my chest, just as I'd felt the bass from the Dillinger album.

The Gary Fisher is a beautiful bike, and I'm sure there are people out there who would think I should get strung up and stung to death by bees or something for messing with it, but those people aren't taking into account the uselessness of a tool you can't operate publicly. If I ride around on a five-thousand-dollar mountain bike, all I'm going to see are eyes staring after me. Everywhere I go I'll be at risk to have it stolen, and that trick with the wrapped chain won't be worth a fistful of pennies.

The Dura-Coat went on really easy, just like the last two times I did this. The paint is only part of the camouflage though—mag wheels and a cheap seat don't hurt either. The mags I'd ordered with the bike, and the seat I'd pick up over the next couple of weeks. When the frame was covered in the matte black and all the other little pieces were dusted, I shut off the compressor and cleaned the airbrush with water. It looked like some half-bit dad had bought some used hunk of junk on the cheap and gave it a quick toss with Krylon to make it cool. Perfect. I left the bike to dry in pieces and went back inside. Almost time to walk to the gas station and make a call.

I ate a couple of spoonfuls of peanut butter out of a jar in the cupboard. I'd cleaned, that was a start, but I seriously needed to go buy some food. I sat at the table with all the funny money spread on it. Totally ridiculous—it looked like a prop from a rap video. If I'd been wearing a sweat suit, had a gold chain and Arrow pinned to my lap, the scene would have been perfect. I stood and tossed the jar of peanut butter in the garbage. It had that oil on top that you're supposed to stir in, and now it had more oil than peanut butter left. I grabbed my hoodie and threw it on, left on foot to call a bad guy.

I dumped three quarters in the phone and dialed the number on the card. I did just like the last time, said "Bark" and the line clicked over. I remembered the breath mints at the last second and tossed three of them in as the man spoke. Wintergreen filled my mouth, and I let him talk.

"Can I help you?"

"We spoke last night about an order."

"Yes. You are in Grand Rapids?"

He said this like I was supposed to be surprised that he could find me; I could hear the smug smile in his voice. Of course I knew he could find me from a phone number, otherwise why would I call from a pay phone? It was an empty threat, just like any I could make; I knew his number was a disposable cell phone.

"Around there."

"I can meet you south of town at the rest stop by mile marker 115."

"When?"

"Two days."

I let impatience sneak into my voice. "Why so long?"

"We have to look into your character. Some men we were dealing with in your area recently got sloppy; I need to know that you don't take those kinds of risks."

Look into my character? I was looking to buy a child, not raise one. Either way, it was just more posturing. He couldn't touch me from where he was; if that were possible, I'd be dealing with him right now. "What time?"

"Eleven p.m. Come alone, and bring the money and your merchandise."

"Alright. How will I know you?"

"You won't. I'll know you. If there is any foolishness, there will be consequences."

"I understand."

"Be sure that you do."

I heard him rattle the phone and punch out of it. I sat down next to the pay phone and let the receiver just hang by my head. I had a place and a time; now I just needed some luck. I left the gas station after hanging up the phone and walked home.

I was restless that night, letting plans formulate and then fade in my head, making my brain a machine, plotting for war and vengeance. Return fire for Shelby, for Arrow, for myself. For Nick and Eleanor, for every kid hurt by an adult. I was going to make these men pay off as much of that debt as they were able, and no matter how much they suffered, it would never be enough.

Chapter 43

I put the bike back together the next morning, more out of neces-sity than desire. People say they're out of food all the time, but I literally was. I worked the bike back into form as quickly as I was able, which really wasn't all that quickly. Disassembly is one thing, construction another. If my last bike had failed me, I'd be dead. Construction has to be perfect. If it was going to fail me, then it wasn't going to be my fault.

Once the last bolt was tightened and the thing stood upright and as beautiful as it could be after my alterations, I tested my weight on it. Things were just fine. If I hadn't known better, I would have thought it was my old one. I went in the house and grabbed my backpack, checked to be sure it was empty, and rode to the grocery store. I checked my watch on the way there—school was out, so I was good to shop.

I ended up buying some pizza rolls, a sack of cheese-filled chicken nuggets, a bunch of those little precut carrots, Carnation instant breakfast, milk, laundry detergent, two loaves of white bread, five boxes of macaroni and cheese, the kind that comes with the cheese pre-made in a foil bag, a jar of peanut butter, two kinds of cereal—not Captain Crunch, I was still recovering—and a pack of trash bags. The lady working the checkout wanted to talk, and I let her go for it, telling her when I was supposed to talk what my mom needed milk for and how my dad would really appreciate it if I could get his beer, too. She laughed and said she couldn't do that, and I said that I knew that, he just seemed to think it would make life easier. We both laughed, and I paid her and took my stuff and hoped I acted enough like a kid. Acting, that's a funny thing. I must be a heck of an actor.

Everything just fit into my backpack. I had a funny feeling the bread probably wouldn't come out looking as nice as it had when it went in, but otherwise it was all in there. I shouldered it and tested the weight before climbing on the bike. If there were a way I could make myself like powdered milk, I'd do it in a heartbeat.

I rode home, and I have to admit, it felt really good. Maybe this bike wasn't exactly like my old one, but it was close. Maybe just a little more tuned, but I knew better than anybody that had nothing to do with my reassembly job. Somebody over at the factory must have figured a way to shave a few more ounces off and reapply them somewhere else. It's a fascinating technology, makes me really interested to wrench on a car. That would be a great summer project in a couple of years, building my first one from the ground up. The trick would be staying alive and free that long. Building the car would be easy by comparison. Even if it came completely disassembled, it would still be easier to construct than my endless stream of charades.

I put away the groceries slowly, killing time like a regular kid assigned some menial task. Lucky for me, I wasn't frustrating some rolling-pin-wielding, ugly-eyed mother with a mean streak. Of course the other side of that coin was kind of a wreck too. I stopped, preheated the oven, and put the rest of the crap away. Already into the pizza rolls—God, I'm so freaking predictable. I'd even promised myself I'd have mac and cheese. Screw it, pizza rolls sounded pretty good. And maybe I was a little worried if I didn't have them now, maybe I never would. I pushed that coldness away. Yeah right.

The oven dinged a few seconds later, and I realized I'd been standing in the kitchen staring at nothing for almost twenty minutes. My head was buzzing. I grabbed an oven mitt and took the pizza rolls from the oven, got a spatula, plated. Let them sit there on the plate—I don't know how they do it, but the filling in those things gets hotter than should be scientifically possible. I've actually researched this, trying to see if there's anything to it. I think it's a big cover-up. The scientists making pizza rolls are using some lava technology to try and burn holes in the roofs of hungry kids' mouths. All I'm missing is a motive. I have a feeling that motive might never get found, and the secret of nuke-temp snack food will never be uncovered.

After I ate, I went to the office and thought about fishing. I'd taken a serious hit money-wise on the bike, and I hadn't been working nearly as much on my scams as I ought to have been. It breaks my heart to think of all the pervs waiting for the right boy and knowing that the *perfect* boy had been too busy to help them have a nice time. I'd make time, just as soon as this was finished.

I left the office, went to the garage, and hopped on the bike. Eighteen pizza rolls shared space with a severe cramping in my belly. If somebody asked me to roll when I got to Rhino's, I was going to explode on them. I wonder if Rhino teaches that? I know it would probably get me to slow down on twisting a limb. Not Rhino, though. He'd probably just eat the sick with a smile on his face. Guess I won't ask him about teaching me that new move.

Chapter 44

I pulled into Rhino's with a smile on my gob. I had to sell a normal boy on helping me look into a monster's face. It would have been nice if I could have asked Rhino, but I can't even imagine the response—the bodies would be stacked like cordwood. Beat one of his fighters in the ring, Rhino would smile, tell you how good you did, no matter what. If you hurt kids, well, that was a whole other story. I'd heard rumors of a couple of different situations involving parents paying to have their kids train in the gym. One of the dads got his arm fully dislocated—arm and shoulder. Like Rhino said, he didn't know the rules, he didn't tap. There are a lot of things I wish for, and one is that I never make Rhino mad.

He's one of the only people who knows the real truth about me, or at least a part of it. He's the only adult I've ever met who not only wouldn't try to help me out, but doesn't think I need to be helped out. He'd been younger than I was when the streets of Curitiba got a taste of him, and he'd never forget it.

I walked in and gave a look around. Jeff was working in the cage and on the ground with Ricardo. Across the gym a couple basketball teams' worth of girls smaller and younger than me by a good bit were dressed in gis and working a nasty Muay-Thai kata. Rhino probably billed it as a Tae-Bo class. All I saw was a thick swarm of smiling, pigtailed killing machines. Two instructors ran the drill, and you could see the murderous force in their hands more clearly than in those of the beaming eight-year-olds. Not that I'd wish any help on the kind of scum that would go after one of them, but the way these girls were training, they could do some serious damage close quarters to throat, groin, or temple. Good.

I crossed the rest of the gym quickly. Rhino's was a good spot to let your eyes wander, but today I wanted to ask Rhino's permission to talk to Jeff, and if he said yes, get out before he could ask me why. I won't lie to him, but he knows when not ask questions. Today he might get those sensors going; maybe I should be asking him. That wouldn't serve the purpose I needed served, though. Violence was one thing, but Rhino's violence would be like bringing a hippo to an art showing at some high-end gallery.

I walked to the door, scanned the gym for him again, and knocked. From inside I heard, "Come in!"

Rhino was sitting behind his desk with an enormous plate of vegetables and raw tuna in front of him. He waved a paw of a hand at the chair. The chopsticks in his fingers looked like my matchsticks by comparison. "Hey, Nickel."

"Hey. I need to ask a favor."

He set the chopsticks down and waved his hands to tell me to speak.

"I'd like to use Jeff on a job tomorrow night. He thinks he owes me something, and I need the transport to get out there. A cab won't work for this."

"You don't ask me for help. Why?"

"The people I'm dealing with, I want them to get in trouble with the police. If they get dead, then the people they deal with will still be free."

He nodded and said, "Dangerous?"

"Yes. But not for Jeff. He's just the wheels."

"Alright. But Nickel? You be careful, really make sure it worth it to get these men to the police instead of, well, instead. They hurt kids, they maybe want to hurt you."

"That's the idea. It's worth the risks."

He smiled and picked up the chopsticks, piled a huge chunk of zucchini into his mouth, chewed, and swallowed it. He said, "You be careful. Come roll soon. You no practice, you lose it, quick."

"I know. I'll be careful, and I'll be back to roll soon. Thank you."

He nodded and got back to the food. I left the office and walked out, past the killer children, now drilling three-punch combinations with their little fingers made into points. Eye, mouth, throat. Eye, mouth, throat. Just like that.

When I got to where Ricardo and Jeff were rolling, I sat and watched. Ricardo was much stronger on the ground than Jeff, but he was leaving himself open to let Jeff clue in on what openings to look for, when to grab a wrist and control it or when to spin out because you were getting yourself in trouble. It was a ballet of almost-violence. They weren't going full speed—Ricardo would ruin Jeff on the ground if they were—but they weren't taking it easy, either. Jeff was getting it.

There are people, Rhino has told me, who boo when a fight hits the ground and yell homophobic insults at the fighters. They're ignorant. To someone tuned into jiu-jitsu and ground fighting, it looks as deadly as two snakes coiled around one another. You can go from winning to losing in seconds. I read that championship-level chess players can really see the pieces getting killed; watching ground fighting can be a lot like that. In sport fighting, you tap. In a street fight, that chokehold might be the last thing you feel.

I watched them go like that for a while, caught in their own little universe. Every few minutes Jeff or Ricardo would stop the other man, and then they'd disconnect and try the same position again, to result in either a more advantageous position or in a submission. I'd rolled before, but never like this. I'd been taught how to street fight. My stuff would never work against a trained opponent who understood the rules, and it would certainly never work in a cage with real rules and a referee. What Ricardo was teaching Jeff would give him the ability to fight at a professional level, if he kept at it and really put his nose down and worked. If today was any indication, Rhino would have Jeff in an amateur fight before the end of the year. Small successes at that level, and the sky was the limit.

Finally they broke. I was almost disappointed—it had been a heck of a show. They stood, shook hands, and embraced, and then they walked towards me and a well-deserved drink of water. Ricardo waved and split; he could tell I needed to talk to Jeff. Jeff sat next to me on the bench and said, "How's it going, Nickel?"

"Good. You look like you're handling yourself well out there."

He grinned. "It's coming slowly to me. Ricardo is amazing, and Rhino's even better. They're good teachers too. What's going on?"

"I need a hand with a job."

"Cool. When?"

"Don't you want to hear about it first?"

"It doesn't matter."

I leaned in a little closer and said, "It could be dangerous."

"That's fine."

"Did you read the paper?"

"Yes. How's the girl?"

"She's alright, about like you'd expect, from what her sister says."

"Are we going after more guys like that?"

"Yes."

"I'm so in."

I told him what he had to do, and when I finished we went over it again. I had trouble calming him down, letting him know how it had to be to go off right. It's hard to get it through to a person training violence every day that they shouldn't just tear a child molester in half, but Jeff got it eventually. By the end he was grinning, ready to make it happen as easy as I said it would be. If only I could be so sure it would be as smooth.

When we were finished, I told him that I'd meet him at the gas station by my house on the following night. He nodded, letting the plan soak in or marinating more on jiu-jitsu—it was tough for me to say. We cracked knuckles, and I went back outside to my replacement bike. I rode home, the pizza rolls settling at about the same rate as the sun by the time I pulled in the driveway.

I read for a little while when I got home, stayed away from the computer as much as possible. I had a plan locked up—the last thing I needed was to wrap my head around something else that would dull my focus. I thought about Arrow and Shelby, and it made me sad. I made a vow to call them in two days when this was over. If I was able to.

I was restless pretty much all day. I ate macaroni and cheese, read for a while, thought about going shopping again for something to do but dismissed the idea after wrestling with it in my head. Finally I decided that if I didn't go for a bike ride, I was going to go nuts. I pulled out of the garage and, for once, didn't go anywhere at all.

I found myself going to all of the usual haunts, I just wasn't stopping. I rode by Riverside but didn't get off the bike to walk around or anything. Remnants of police tape hung from a tree by where the shooting had happened. It made me feel cold on the inside and like a little kid on the outside. I could feel Shelby on my shoulder, feel the bullets tugging at the wind around us—only in my head, Eyepatch wasn't there and we were dead on the lawn. I could still call this whole thing off, just not show up and be done with it. Thought about that some more. No, I couldn't.

I rolled out to Four Oaks, passed by Arrow's house but didn't stop. There was a For Sale sign in the front yard. It made my chest feel like my lungs were full of gummy bears. I rode past it, trying not to think about what that meant. I could not deal. I rode home as fast as I could to call Arrow.

"Hello."

"It's me. How are you?"

"I was going to tell you. It just happened. Shel...my sister is more messed up than they thought at first. Like, really messed up. We're going to move to an apartment until the house sells."

"In town?"

I could hear her swallow thickly over the phone. "No. Milwaukee."

I didn't know what to say. My lips worked independently of the rest of me and spoke anyways. The word came out like cold ketchup from a glass jar: "When?"

"Soon. Movers are coming tomorrow."

"Are you moving tomorrow?"

"No. Probably the day after. Maybe the next one after that. You'd really have to ask my folks."

My mouth kept working on its own. Nothing I'd ask her folks would be polite. "I have to work tonight. Would you want to come over tomorrow?"

"To your house?"

"Yeah. I could make us dinner; we can just hang out for a little bit."

"Like a date?"

"I'm too young to date."

"So am I, but if I say it's a date, it's a date."

"Alright."

I seriously don't know how I was even talking—my mouth felt like it was full of cotton, and my blood had turned to molasses.

"What are you going to cook?"

"Steaks. Sound okay?"

"It sounds wonderful."

"I'll send Lou over to pick you up from the gas station by your house tomorrow. Five okay?"

"That would be perfect."

"See you then."

She hung up.

Crap. Why steaks? Of all things, why did my dumb mouth put in a stellar performance only to kill it by offering to cook the one thing that I could not cook? I ran to the computer, did a search for steak, how to cook steak, the perfect steak, all kinds of stuff. Every search had the same link at the top of the page for a place called Lobel's. I broke and checked out the site. According to them, they sold the best meat in the U.S. I ordered two rib eyes for overnight delivery. With shipping, it was just shy of a hundred bucks. I figure if I burn them too bad, I'll show her the receipt for sympathy. How could I be more worried about that than tonight? Tonight was a war—tomorrow was aged beef. I looked at the clock on the computer. Time to get ready for them. As scared as I was, I couldn't wait to look in their eyes and see the fear well up.

Chapter 45

Inside, I was ready for war; outside, I looked like I'd just left one. My camouflage was poverty: I wore my most threadbare, tight jeans and had on a hoodie with nothing underneath it. I wanted to look like the kid I could have been if I hadn't escaped, a sad, used-up little mess of a boy. Even my hair was a little mussed with gel. That had been hard because I don't have much hair. If they searched me, they wouldn't find anything but an ink pen. If they really got to work searching, there might be problems. I didn't think they would. Every factor I could control had been handled; now I just had to let it play. I chewed a matchstick, my third once since I'd gotten to the gas station. It was cold out, and I invited the weather in, let it get bone deep, let it show on my face. I was raw, scraped all the way down, and that was perfect.

Jeff showed up after I'd been there about an hour. He was early. He got out of the car and sat next to me on the curb, and I shuffled the duffle with the money over to him. He grabbed it and set it on his lap. He said, "Are you ready?"

I nodded a response. We sat in silence for about fifteen minutes and stood together. We walked to his car and got in, and a few minutes later we were on the highway, headed south. When I saw a sign for the rest stop, I clambered over the seats to sit in the back. He pulled in and parked at the edge of the lot by the trees. There were two semi trucks parked on the other side and a car pulling out as we'd pulled in, but otherwise the place was a ghost town. Jeff got out and sat on the hood, the bag with the funny money still in the car.

I watched the black Lincoln pull in and park three spots down from us. The windows were tinted, and I could see nothing inside of it.

The person on the passenger side got out. It was a man, I could tell by how he was walking, but I would have been shocked by anything else. He was big. He approached Jeff and said something. Jeff nodded and knocked a thumb at the car. They were either talking about the money or me. Jeff walked to the passenger side door and opened it, took the money and set it on the hood. I took the pen and tucked it into my sock. The man opened the bag, fiddled around for a few minutes, and zipped it up. They exchanged a few more words, and the man brought the money to the Lincoln and tossed it in the trunk. Jeff came back to the passenger side door, opened it, and said, "Get out."

I did. I walked in front of Jeff and stopped in front of the car with the man. He grabbed my shoulder and spun me, letting his eyes creep over me.

Jeff said, "Whaddya think, he cover it? He's clean, man, super clean, long gone. He's put in work, but always supervised, you know? You could turn him out, party, whatever." Jeff was acting like a total meathead. It was perfect.

The man said, "He'll do."

He walked to the car, opened the rear driver's side door, and yanked out a little brunette girl, maybe seven or eight years old. If I'd brought Rhino, this is where it would've gotten really bad. I could see the tears on her face in the moonlight. She was dressed like a streetwalking prostitute. The man led her to Jeff and said, "This is Cindy. Cindy, this is the man I told you about, okay?"

"I want to go home."

Jeff brought her around the car and helped her in the back seat. If there was a home, and it was a good place, she'd get to go there. If not, she'd wind up somewhere okay. Rhino knew a cop who actually cared about stuff like that, checked up to be sure, the kind of cop who wouldn't let a pair of predators make kids into movie stars. The man snapped me back to attention, grabbed my shoulder, gave me a shake. He pointed at the car and shoved me towards the door. I got in, making sure not to look back at Jeff. He had his instructions; all he had to do was follow them. I watched his car pull out and leave the rest area. The man got back in the car, and the other man stared back at me. He had white hair and spoke in a high, reedy voice. He smiled at me. He looked like a shark that smelled blood. "Ready to have some fun?"

I nodded, looking as solemn as possible. I buckled in the middle seat and gave myself slack so I could move. The two men smiled, and the car backed out and hopped on the highway, jumped on the first ramp, and turned around to head back to the city. The two men in the front spoke, but I couldn't really hear them over the radio. I looked to the front seat. We were doing just over seventy. I took the pen from my pocket and held the top to unscrew it, and then I pushed my arm over the front seat between the headrests. One of them grabbed my arm. I closed my eyes, took a deep breath, and pressed the button. Mace filled the car.

The air was fire—rancid, smoking fire. The car was all over the road, dancing back and forth. I kept my eyes closed and fought fear in the darkness. Took my left shoe off, peeled off the sole, and felt for the little bottle of mineral oil. I poured the contents on my sock and yanked the wet thing off of my foot, ran it over my eyes and in my nostrils. I opened my eyes just as the car went off the road and flipped.

We rolled twice, and I bounced hard when we stopped. I shook the cobwebs out and grabbed my right shoe. The big guy who'd been outside was sleeping, but the driver was moving, hands already clawing at his seat belt. I didn't have much time. I tore off my right shoe and peeled the sole from it. The driver was climbing over the seat, screaming curses at me. The syringe fumbled in my fingers. He grabbed my injured arm and wrenched on it; my world went gray and then snapped back. He was almost over the seat. Ignoring him as best I was able, I focused on my right hand; the left felt numb and detached. I grabbed the first syringe and stuck it in his mouth as he toppled over the seat. Pushed the plunger and gave him enough Ketamine to put down a small horse. Just enough to maybe not kill him.

He flailed at the syringe for a moment and then bent at the waist and just got gone, half in the front seat, half in the back. I took the other syringe and bent over the seat, stuck it in the big guy's neck to help him sleep. I dropped the note I'd typed in the front seat on his lap. I didn't figure he'd read it, but it ought to give the fuzz some probable cause beyond the loaded dough in the trunk.

Chapter 46

When I finally pulled myself out of the car, my head was just banging. The car was in worse shape: the frame was bent, the whole car looked like someone with a bad disposition had worked it over with a mallet and sandpaper. I gave myself a look. I'd been better. My arm felt like it was going to come off, and the rest of me wasn't a whole lot better. It was going to be bad when the adrenaline dump wore off.

I opened the driver's door and popped the trunk. Leaned back in and turned the car off. Went to the trunk and took fifty thousand in fake hundreds, then zipped the bag and looked around the trunk. There was another little duffle in there. Nice—as was the fact that I now wouldn't be covering the back end on the counterfeit bucks. Here's the thinking: leaving the funny money in the car with the bad guys would make the cops think they already had a closed case. They'd just figure any other money that started showing up had already been distributed from the batch they'd found, which I guess it had been—to me.

I threw the bag over my shoulder and closed the trunk, walked into the woods at the side of the road, and got moving back to the rest stop. I needed to be well clear by the time the cops showed up. Looking down the highway I could see four or five sets of taillights, cars stopping to call for help.

I tucked the money into the wide pocket in my hoodie and tried not to think about what had just happened or about the adrenaline. I walked through the woods and listened for sirens. In a few minutes, I heard them. I ran, crushing pine needles and leaves—fall was falling.

I walked from the trees and onto asphalt. Stuck a matchstick in my teeth, adjusted the bag I took from the trunk on my shoulder, and walked into the yellow light buzzing from the streetlights. I could see Jeff sitting on the hood of his car looking worried. I walked over to him.

"Nickel! God, you just scared the crap out of me. Where'd you come from?"

I pointed to the woods and threw the duffle on the hood next to Jeff. Unzipping it I saw that it was full of exactly what I'd expected: money. No surprise, really—guys like that would have a hard time using a regular bank. I took out two bricks of bills and handed them to Jeff. "One for you, one for Rhino."

"Where'd you get this?"

"The trunk. How is she?"

"Scared out of her head."

I grabbed the duffle, opened the car door, got in, and sat next to her. Jeff got in after me and turned the car on. The girl wasn't saying anything, just sitting there shaking. I said, "Cindy?"

She looked at me with these big, terrified blue eyes. "I want to go home."

"I know, but listen, you're going to have to talk to the police first, go to the hospital and make sure you're okay. Jeff is going to say he found you walking by the side of the road. You need to pretend that those bad guys were driving somewhere and crashed. You got out and walked until Jeff found you. Everything else you tell them can be true. Can you do that?"

She nodded her head. I took her hand, and she leaned into me—it was a little painful, to be honest, but if it made her feel even a little better it was okay with me. I let my breath out, let the terror back in. Let the fear shake through me. I'd gone back into the lion's den and come out alive. By the time we got to my gas station, Cindy was asleep. I slipped Cindy off of my shoulder, made sure she was comfortable, gave Jeff a wave, and then took the duffel and waited until they left. I had calls to make, but they could wait until morning. I walked home smiling.

Chapter 47

Knocking on the door woke me. I almost ran for the rear exit when I remembered the steaks. I looked at the clock: 7:30 a.m. I answered the door and took a package from the FedEx guy, signed his slip, and he was gone. The package was big but lighter than it looked. That was a good thing; I felt terrible. Inside the box were two gorgeous rib eyes, a little catalog/instruction manual, and some ice packs. I threw the cooler into the garage and put the steaks in the fridge. I had nine and a half hours until Arrow came over. Nine and a half hours to learn how not to ruin a hundred bucks worth of steaks. I went to the garage and hopped on my bike. The shower could wait.

I remembered that I'd made myself look like crap the night before when I was halfway to the grocery store. Too far now to turn around. I went in and bought two huge potatoes, a pack of unsalted butter, a little tub of sour cream, extra virgin olive oil, and six rib eye steaks. The lady working kind of gave me a look, and I said, "My mom is scared the roast won't be big enough."

She nodded as if that explained away a kid grocery shopping before school perfectly. For all I know, it does. I crammed all of the crap in my backpack and raced out of there. Got home and grabbed the little book that had come with the mail steaks and set it on the counter while I put the rest of the food away. I put the steaks in the fridge along with the butter and sour cream. Left the potatoes and oil on the counter and got to reading. First thing on the list, get steaks to room temp. Crap. I took four of the grocery store rib eyes out and set them on the counter.

I used a paring knife to remove the plastic wrap and put all four steaks on a metal serving tray. I went and got the salt and pepper out and was about to douse them when I grabbed the book. Don't season until ready to grill. I left them on the counter and went to check the computer.

Local news site had the arrest and the counterfeit bits. Left out Cindy entirely, but did say that the men were believed to have been involved in several kidnappings. The cops found two more kids at their house, one of them dead. It made it sound like the two guys from the car were alive—good. I took a deep breath and left the computer. So far my end was clean. So far.

I went back to the kitchen and checked my steaks. They were getting close, so I did like the book said and got the grill started. I rubbed the grates down with olive oil and went back in to let the thing heat up.

I read step three in the little guidebook and seasoned the meat. I only did one of the steaks and then read that I needed to brush them with olive oil in the middle of cooking. I tucked the guide in my back pocket, poured some oil in a little bowl, dropped in a silicone grilling brush, and brought the bowl and the steak outside. The grill was ready.

I dropped the steak on the fire using tongs, like the book said. I'm not a dummy, I knew not to use a fork already, but it was nice to have that reaffirmed. I seared it just like the book said, brushed it down with oil, and flipped it. When I was done, I had something that resembled an oblong hockey puck, only less appetizing. It was almost three o'clock before my steaks were coming out right. I left the grill on—it's a good thing it hooks to the house line, or I'd be screwed. I can't imagine lugging a propane tank on my bike. I went in the house and prepped the potatoes. Poked them full of holes with a fork, rubbed them all over with olive oil, and seasoned them. I put the potatoes on the grill, took a shower, and made some calls.

Gary answered like he'd been waiting on me. "Hello?"

"Hey."

"Oh hey man, what's up?"

"Not much."

Yeah right.

"I'm going to be making a drop in our spot, funny money, fifty stacks."

"What's the word?"

"Get rid of it."

"For free?"

"Yeah, but tell the folks who get it to spend it."

"Why?"

"Don't worry about it."

"Okay. When?"

"I'll drop off tonight, late."

"I'll be ready to go soon man, one more week."

"Good. Get it spread good, Gary, all social circles. Word for anybody busted, dude with white hair handed it out."

"Alright."

I hung up, two more calls to make.

"Hello?"

"It's done."

"When..."

"Tonight, after midnight. Same spot as last time."

"Is it…"

"Not yet. Give it a week before you do whatever you were planning to do. I've got money running on a couple of different angles for you."

I hung up, called Lou. Told him where, who, and when. He didn't say a word, just listened and hung up. I went back in the kitchen, took the steaks out of the fridge, and opened them up. They looked and smelled different than the ones from the store, richer. I'd been eating steak all day, and I was still excited. I put the meat on a plate and went into the living room. I sat on the couch and tried to read for about a half an hour, but then I gave up and walked to the gas station.

Chapter 48

I'd been sitting for about twenty minutes when Arrow and Lou showed up. She got out, beautiful in a pair of jeans and a black hooded sweatshirt, hair piled atop her head like a mess of spaghetti and held together with a clip. Lou poled an arm out of the driver's side window. I paid him a fifty and said, "Keep it, for next time. I'll call in a few hours."

Lou nodded, a long conversation for us, and drove off. I walked to Arrow and said, "Are you ready?"

"Are you sure you want to do this?"

"What do you mean?"

"Like, show me your house and stuff. If you changed your mind, I wouldn't be offended."

"I want you to see my house. No one else ever has."

We got to walking, right into my little nest of improvised suburbia. I showed her my first drop box as we passed it, told her how I built it, and she nodded like she was impressed. For all I know, she really was. I stopped when we got to the house. "Here we are."

"This house?"

"Yeah, what's wrong with it?"

"It's just so, well, normal."

"What did you expect, a tree fort clubhouse?"

Her face reddened. I felt my heart trying to rip its way out of my chest.

"No…I'm not sure. Actually, kind of. This is nice. Really nice. Really normal, but nice."

"You want to see the inside?"

"Yes, I do."

I bent over like an old-timey butler and extended my arm. "Then let's go."

I let her sashay in front of me, jogging ahead at the last minute to open the door. Arrow stepped around me and into my house. She said, "Where's all your stuff?"

"What do you mean?"

I looked at my living room, outfitted with a couch and nothing, leading to a kitchen and dining room with a card table and four chairs. I guess it was sparse. To be honest, I'd never really cared until now.

"You…don't have a TV?"

"Too slow, too dumb."

She nodded. God, I love this girl. "That actually makes sense. What's in there?"

"Bedroom this way, office that way."

"Are those our steaks?"

"Yeah, why?"

"They look amazing! Did you get those at Meijer's?"

"No, Lobe something. Online."

"You ordered us steaks from Lobel's?"

"Yeah. Wait, those are good, right? Because seriously, it didn't put me out or anything, but I spent a pile on…"

"How did you know about Lobel's? I barely even know about that, and that was only because some idiot buddy of my dad's wouldn't shut up about them at some stupid party."

"Just a guess."

"Let's put them on the grill. Is it hot?"

"Yes ma'am."

"Get the steaks, dummy."

We walked outside, me leading Arrow, holding a plate full of steaks and shouldering salt and pepper. I wasn't sure what to say about the corn, so I just let her go for it. "You have a farm!"

"Yep."

"Just corn?"

"Sort of."

She ducked her head in and yanked it back faster than it went in. "You grew that pot?"

"Yes."

I opened the grill, tossed black pepper on the steaks, oiled the grates again, and fired the meat. Flames roared, and I shot Arrow a smile, shut the grill. I looked at my watch, noted the time, and said, "Five minutes."

"Aren't you scared you'll get caught?"

"Yes."

"So why…"

"I have to make money somehow, and I figure it's not really hurting anybody. I charge a fair price and make a pretty good product. Everybody wins."

Arrow walked away from me, to the side of the corn and weed plot, and said, "I don't want to move. I have like three friends who would let me stay with them, and my mom even says it would be okay if I want to, but when I mentioned it in front of Shelby, she wouldn't stop screaming. I hate to say this, but sometimes I wish she would've just died. It doesn't seem fair for her to live through something like that just to be so messed up by it that she can't live a normal life."

I balanced my words like people level a checkbook. "It'll take a while for her to come around, and a lot of that is going to have to do with Shelby, not counseling or meds or anything."

I almost told her about me, the real story, but I shut that off just as quick as it started. The house was one thing, but I couldn't go that far. For better or worse, the survivor—the secrets, the sins, mine or others—always wins. She got the edited version.

"I had a super messed-up childhood. My dad died when I was young, and I bounced around foster care before and after that. Now I just try not to think about all that stuff and just live as good as I can. There are worse things out there than surviving, but sometimes it's hard to know that I was able to come through it okay when so many kids don't. That's why I do what I do. Not every kid that falls through the cracks needs to stay down there."

I opened the grill, flipped the steaks, and painted them with olive oil. I took the potatoes off and placed them on a clean plate. Four minutes, final stretch.

"You live the craziest life of anyone I ever met. Pretty much every kid I know would kill to live like you, but they'd all just waste it. You aren't messing it up. It's like we know some secret."

"Arrow. Trust me, no one wants to live like me."

"I could stay with you. We could help people together, like you did with Shelby."

I wanted to say yes, we'll be crime-fighting buddies and you'll live here and when I turn eighteen we'll marry and be the world's all-time greatest private investigating couple. Instead, I said, "The steaks ought to be done. You hungry?"

"Yeah."

I pulled the steaks off of the grill and flopped them onto the plate with the potatoes. I shut the grill off with supreme confidence, but I had a day of ruined meat behind me. I slid the door open and gestured to Arrow. She glided in the house in front of me and shut the door behind me. I pulled the potatoes off of the plate and set them on matching vessels. I tossed a piece of aluminum foil over the steaks to allow them to tent. According to the guide, this lets the juices flow back in. I didn't care what it did—if that guide said do it, I was doing it. I handed Arrow one of the plates with a potato on it, grabbed us knives and forks, and set a stick of butter and the sour cream on the table. I took the plates with the steaks and gestured to the table, got my potato and plate in my other hand, and sat. I set my potato in front of me and the steaks in the center of the table. I said, "Let's eat."

That's exactly what we did. I won't say that I'd trust myself to just make steaks on the fly in the future, but I did a nice job with those ones. I'm sure part of it was the meat, but part of it had to be the chef, right?

Chapter 49

After my steak was about three-quarters gone and my potato was nothing but a jacket, I pushed my plate away from me. Arrow winked and gave me a thumbs-up, and then she soldiered on until her steak was gone. The darkness was creeping in the windows. When she finished, I took our plates and dumped what was left of mine in the garbage. Arrow's plate went right to the sink. She said, "You said you couldn't make steaks, you big liar! That was awesome."

I grinned. "They did turn out pretty good."

"Heck yeah."

"You have to go soon."

"I know. I don't want to."

"I don't want you to."

She gave me a sad, crooked little smile, the kind that says, "I'll sure miss you, but if my sister had never been taken, we never would have met and my life would be normal."

"I'll call Lou."

"He's a funny guy."

"How do you mean?"

"He wouldn't stop talking the whole way over here."

Freaking Lou, more secrets than me.

196

I showed her my phones, explained how they worked, and she at least pretended to be impressed. I let her call Lou, and when she was done we walked to the gas station. We didn't talk. I hate that. I guess there was nothing else to say. We sat together on the curb to wait for Lou. After a few minutes, he showed. Arrow grabbed me hard, held on for a minute, and then peeled back, kissed me full on the lips, and shoved me away.

"Thank you for everything. I'll see you again."

"You know where to find me."

She smiled. My Arrow.

She got in the car. I walked to Lou and handed him a fold of money. "For next time."

He nodded. They left. My heart broke. I went home.

Song at the End of the Show

So then, if you're reading this, you must have liked it. The first thanks go to you, for giving me a chance. I'd like to ask a favor, and if you agree to it, then here we go.

We're in a club, and either Frank Turner is playing the wonderful break where he addresses the crowd in "Photosynthesis," Green Day is doing their own break in "Paper Lanterns," or The Hold Steady is playing "Your Little Hoodrat Friend." In any case, in our version, the singer is pontificating—that would be me—and the bass player and drummer are playing the nearly unforgettable rhythm bits of those songs ad nauseam. The guitar player looks bored—maybe he's drinking a beer or lighting a cigarette. Seriously, I've seen all of these wonderful bands do this, and the convictions in maintaining the song is just jaw dropping. The front man is talking, massaging the crowd, but they're ready for him to say 1-2-3-4 at any given second. They're on edge, but they'd never admit it.

Are you with me? Can you hear the bass, feel the drums?

I want to thank my dear family for putting up with me, especially my wife and daughter for dealing with the mood swings that come part and parcel when you deal with a wannabe author who will neither quit nor accept rejection.

I want to thank my father for dealing with manuscript after manuscript, short story after short story, mostly terrible, but you always read them.

My mother said not to give up, and I guess she was right. I still can't believe that I didn't.

Cheers to my friends the Mazureks, boys and adults. Cheers to my fellows at Mos Eisleys, who know more than anyone how much sweat creation takes.

Thanks go to Lukas, who read it first, and Greg, who read it second.

A deep thanks to Terry, who made me shout with joy in my basement, pour a good beer in my favorite glass, and throw a laptop in front of my wife to read the kind of letter that I'd long ago given up on getting. To Sarah, who introduced herself and said she was going to help me market my book, another hands-shaking, nearly-pass-out moment. To David, who did everything I ever could have dreamed an editor would do, and never thought that they would. To Jessica, who did the copy edit on *Nickel Plated* and helped me through the last steps.

To AmazonEncore, for giving me a chance. To everyone else who worked on this thing behind the scenes.

The bass player looks bored, people are getting drinks—I'm almost done, I swear.

To you, and I mean it. I hope we talk again. I know Nickel would love that. The amplifiers are buzzing, the room is restless, the bar and the bathrooms are beckoning. "1-2-3-4!"

About the Author

Megan Davis, Silver Gallery Photography, 2010

Aric Davis is married with one daughter and lives in Grand Rapids, Michigan, where he has worked for the past fourteen years as a body piercer. A punk rock aficionado, Davis does anything he can to increase awareness of a good band. He likes weather cold enough to need a sweatshirt but not a coat, and friends who wear their hearts on their sleeves. In addition to reading and writing, he also enjoys roller coasters and hockey. *Nickel Plated* is his debut novel.